000572642

D0405618

Jackson County Library System
Medford, OR 97501

r804

DATE DUE			
JAN 12 '96	SEP 21 '01		
JUN 20 '96	SEP 18 '04		
AUG 6 '96			
SEP 13 '96			
OCT 3 '96	7-21		
MAY 1 5 '97			
SEP 1 2 '97			
SEP 2 3 '97			
OCT 1 4 '99			
OCT 2 5 '00			
MAY 4 - '01			
MAY 1 7 '01			

w/0
✓ 01

Jackson

County

Library

System

SEP 1 5 1995

HEADQUARTERS:

413 W. Main

Medford, Oregon   97501

GAYLORD M2G

PASSIN'
THROUGH

PASSIN' THROUGH

LOUIS L'AMOUR

BANTAM BOOKS
NEW YORK • TORONTO • LONDON • SYDNEY • AUCKLAND

JACKSON COUNTY LIBRARY SYSTEM
MEDFORD, OREGON 97501

PASSIN' THROUGH

A Bantam Book / October 1985
Louis L'Amour Hardcover Collection edition / October 1985

All rights reserved.
Copyright © 1985 by Louis L'Amour Enterprise, Inc.
Book designed by Renée Gelman.
This book may not be reproduced in whole or in part, by
mimeograph or any other means, without permission.
For information address: Bantam Books, Inc.

ISBN 0-553-06301-4

Published simultaneously in the United States and Canada

Bantam Books are published by Bantam Books, a division
of Bantam Doubleday Dell Publishing Group, Inc. Its trademark, consisting of the words "Bantam Books" and the
portrayal of a rooster, is Registered in U.S. Patent and
Trademark Office and in other countries. Marca Registrada.
Bantam Books, 1540 Broadway, New York, New York 10036.

PRINTED IN THE UNITED STATES OF AMERICA

0 9 8 7 6 5 4 3 2

To Stan and Mary,
To Mutt and Fern
who live in the shadow of Maggie.

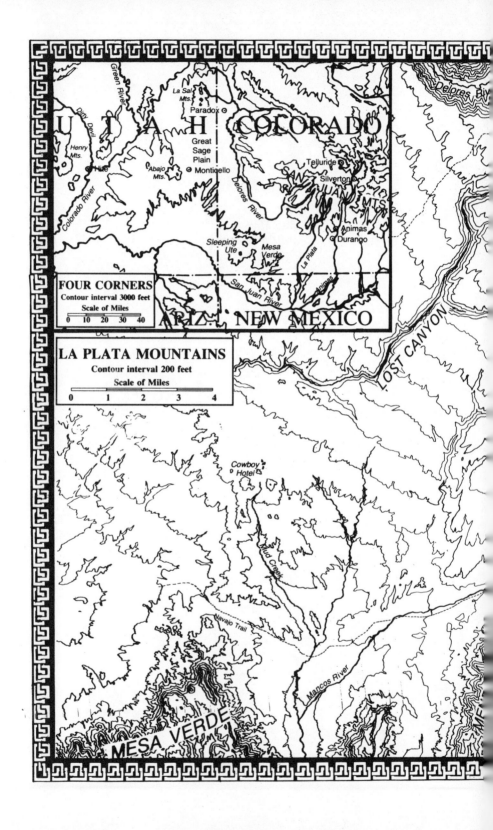

FOUR CORNERS
Contour interval 3000 feet
Scale of Miles
0 10 20 30 40

LA PLATA MOUNTAINS
Contour interval 200 feet
Scale of Miles
0   1   2   3   4

UTAH

COLORADO

Green River

La Sal Mts.

Paradox

Dirty Devil

Henry Mts.

Great Sage Plain

Hite

Colorado River

Abajo Mts.

Monticello

Delores River

Telluride

SAN JUAN MTS

Silverton

Animas

Durango

Sleeping Ute

Mesa Verde

La Plata

San Juan River

Animas

ARIZ. NEW MEXICO

Delores River

LOST CANYON

Cowboy Hotel

Mud Creek

Navajo Trail

Mancos River

MESA VERDE

Map by Alan McKnight

AUTHOR'S NOTE

Parrott City is no more. Cattle graze where the town once stood, and thick stands of Gambel oak have replaced the hastily constructed buildings that once occupied the site. Occasional deer browse where the eating house stood, and the town site is part of a ranch, privately owned.

The town began as did many western towns, with planks laid across the tops of two barrels of whiskey in the shade of some trees. By all accounts, business was good from the moment they opened the first barrel.

When Clubfoot found his mine somewhere high on Madden Peak or in the vicinity, it was the Dutchman who melted down the gold and kept Clubfoot's secret until after his death. Many have searched for his mine but it remains undiscovered, although other claims have been located that might be outcroppings of the same vein.

The La Platas are a lovely range of mountains, their highest peaks rising to over thirteen thousand feet, and several of the others topping twelve thousand, their flanks cloaked with a heavy growth of spruce, ponderosa pine, and aspen. The La Plata River begins here, as do the several branches of the Mancos, and I've been to the sources of them all at one time or another.

The yellow-bellied marmots such as seen by Passin' are still common, as are deer, elk, bear, and mountain lion. There are trails fit for a four-wheel-drive vehicle, but mostly it is hiking country, if you are accustomed to high altitudes. Much gold and silver was found here in the past and several mines are still working.

The Spanish worked placers along the La Plata, and the first mine opened by an American was in 1873. The first permanent settlers arrived in 1875, making this one of the last areas to be settled outside of Alaska. The Spanish came early and left their names on the land, and then there were the miners, cattlemen, sheepmen, and the railroaders. A few of each remain, as do the Indians, Utes, Jicarilla Apaches, and the Navajo, all close by.

On a late afternoon when the clouds gather around the peaks and the lightning begins to play its games over the mountain meadows, the high country is no place to be, but it can be spectacular to watch from a safe distance. At such times the hills can be alive with a sound that isn't music, but it has a magnificence of its own.

ONE

Behind me a noose hung empty and before me the land was wild.

I rode a blue horse to the trail's divide and tossed a coin to choose my way. The coin fell left and I turned the roan, but doubt rode my shoulders like an evil thing.

The rimrock broke and the trail dipped through the crack, and my horse picked a careful way to the bottom, down the earth and rockslide that lay below the notch. Sweat stung my neck where the rope burns were, for the flesh was torn and raw. At the bottom of the slide I turned left again and the roan moved eagerly forward.

There would be riders behind me now, eager to hang me again, for they were fierce and bitter men with hatred for me, a stranger.

Yet when had I not been a stranger, riding alone?

There had been nothing ahead to look to, and nothing behind I wanted to remember, so I'd headed west into new country simply because it was new country. Wild and reckless and hard I was, and quick with a gun to shoot, with a face honed down by sun, wind, and hardship, and eyes, some said, like chunks of blue ice.

When I came upon them standing beside the trail I was headed for a far-off town. An Indian woman with an Indian boy, an old man and a horse dead beside them.

They lifted no hand and made no sign, but the look of trouble was harsh upon them. The desert lay wide around them, a desolate land where no water was. Turning my horse, I rode to where they stood, and their lips were parched and cracked. The boy's eyes went to my canteen but he said nothing.

1

They stood and looked at me and I took the canteen from its lashings and passed it to the woman. She passed it first to the boy and he took it and drank, then returned it to her.

From the last of my hoarded biscuits I gave them food, then helped to bury the old man, safe from wolves and buzzards.

Then I put them up on my packhorse and carried them to the town, where I gave each a silver dollar. I stabled my horses, stowed my gear in the corner of a dusty, rarely used tack room, and walked to the saloon for a drink. A bad choice in a bad town.

There was a tall man at the bar, a man with a mustache and goatee, his black coat drawn back to reveal a pearl-handled gun. A mean man, a cruel man, a man looking for trouble, and here was I, a stranger.

When I saw his face I knew his kind and went to the far end of the bar. Heat and weariness had shortened my temper so I wanted space about me and no words with anyone until I had eaten and rested.

He stared at me and said, "Afraid of something?"

"Of nothing," I said, and there was impatience in my tone, for I knew what was coming. There was in me the memory of other such towns and other such men.

"You are not polite," he said, "and I like people to be polite when they speak to me. Do you know who I am?"

"Leave me alone," I said. "I shall be gone within the hour."

The bartender poured my drink and there was a warning in his eyes.

"Do you know who I am?" he persisted.

Tiredness and impatience overruled my judgment. "A damned fool if you persist in this," I said. "I'm a drifting man who just wants to drift."

"A 'damned fool' he calls me, and he's wearing a gun, too." He dropped his hand to his gun and I killed him.

His gun had not cleared leather when my bullet took him at the base of the throat, and there was a moment when his face was wild with disbelief. He had killed before but he had not expected to die. He looked into my eyes with all the manhood gone from his. He sank to his knees and he tried to speak but blood was choking him, and he went face-down in the sawdust, filling his clutching fists with it.

"You will hang for this," someone said, "hang until you're dead!"

"He was asking for it. He put a hand to his gun before I did."

"It makes no difference. He is a known man and you are not. There's his brother behind you with a shotgun now."

So they took me out, his brothers did, and hanged me high from a cottonwood limb. There was no drop to break my neck, for they shoved me off the rump of a blue roan horse and left me strangling there, to die slowly while they went off for a drink.

Then the Indian woman and the boy came from the brush and cut me down. They removed the noose from my neck and stood by while I gagged and choked and coughed. The blue roan horse stood there and on him was a fine saddle with a rifle in the scabbard.

My own horses were a mile away in a livery stable and to get them I'd have to go through town. Taking up the bridle reins, I put a foot in the stirrup, and the Indian woman said, "No! No!"

She gestured violently. "Bad! Horse no good! Bad! Bad!"

"He may be bad but he's the only one I've got. My horses and gear are in the stable and I'm not going back there." Swinging to the saddle, I turned to give them my thanks but they had turned their backs on me and were disappearing into the brush.

The roan moved out eagerly and I let him go. "You've a smart way about you, Horse," I said, "and I like it."

From the scabbard I shucked the Winchester and checked the magazine . . . fully loaded. My pistols needed no checking, picked from the ground where they had been thrown and handed to me by the Indian boy when they took the noose from my neck.

There was one empty shell and I let it fall to the ground as I thumbed in another cartridge. So small a thing to empty out a man's life.

The trail branched but the horse went left and I let him go. Left it began and left it could continue, although I regretted the outfit left behind, and the horse as well, although he was no such a horse as this I rode.

Dust devils danced where the hot sun lay, and heat waves shimmered in the distance. Mountains lay west and behind me, blue mountains with a hint of pines upon them, but my horse stepped south and east, tossing his head and eager for the distance. He had style, that horse did, and no doubt his owner would be riding with the posse that would follow.

It was a wide land, an empty land, with a vast distance before the mountains came, mountains that knuckled against the sky like doubled fists. Clouds gathered there, hinting of the late-afternoon rains that came often to these hills.

Glancing back, I saw no dust. Yet I knew the manner of men they were, and they would be coming to hang me again and this time they would not fail. Escape I must, or fight, and they would be too many for me. Yet I did not run the roan because he was too fine a horse to kill, and the heat was great.

When I looked back along my trail the roan turned from it into the sagebrush. He seemed to know where he was going so I let him have his head. He might know where there was good water and I did not.

The distant mountains toward which I rode were beginning to take shape from the haze and gathering shadows. I looked back again, and saw no dust.

What was wrong? Could it be possible they did not know I had escaped their hanging? Knowing western men and their towns, I'd have bet a shirt they would be on my trail within the hour. Or did they know something I did not and were riding by some other route to head me off? Was I riding into a trap?

How far had I come? Fifteen miles? Twenty? What I needed now was a camp, even if I had no blankets, no food, and no water. The roan needed rest as I did, and moreover, I needed to know where I was going. In the gathering dark all was mystery.

Once when I moved to turn off the dim trail the roan objected and pulled away. "What's the matter, boy? Do you know something I don't?"

Suddenly, almost a mile further along, the roan turned from the trail and followed a creek into the hills. "Hope you know what you're doin', Horse," I said, "because I sure don't."

He wound around, went along a flat through some cedars, and suddenly dipped down and headed into the darkness where trees clustered against a rock shelf. Behind the trees he stopped.

A moment I sat the saddle listening. There was no sound but the ripple of water and occasionally a stirring of the leaves. Overhead the stars were disappearing behind drifting clouds. In the distance there was a rumble of thunder.

On my left there seemed to be a black opening of some sort.

Carefully, I dismounted and, holding the reins, moved toward the wide, dark opening.

No sound. I took a chance and struck a match, holding it up. A cave! Not a deep cave, but a place where water seemed to have hollowed a natural shelter. It was empty.

Leading the roan inside, I tied him to a projecting horn of rock and gathered sticks from under the trees, hoping I would not also gather a snake. When I had a few sticks I got a fire started and looked around. The cave was about twenty feet across, at a rough guess, and something more than half that deep. On one side there had been a rockfall, a slab dropping from the roof overhead.

The place where I'd started my fire was an old, well-used fireplace. Looking around again, I swore softly. I knew this place! Not from memory, but from word passed along the trail. It was called the Cowboy Hotel and dozens of drifting or passing cowboys had spent nights here. It was a convenient shelter with water and fuel. If I was right, there was grass on the meadow just beyond the trees. Not very good grass but forage for a hungry horse.

Taking the rope from the saddle, I picketed the roan on the grass close to the water. He drank, looked at me with his ears forward, and I talked softly to him. "I've a hunch you and me are two of a kind," I said. "One thing I want you should know. I done a lot of things but I never stole no horse before." I straightened up from gathering fuel and thought about it. No, none that I could recall. Of course, when a man's in a hurry . . .

Whose horse was he, anyway? Why hadn't they led him away after using him to hang me? Puzzled, I lit a small torch and walked over to where the horse stood. He looked at me, rolling his eyes at the fire. "It's all right, boy. I just want to look at your brand."

It was on his left hip. I looked and then looked again. That was a hell of a brand to put on a good horse! A hell of a brand. *A skull and crossbones.*

Backing off, I looked at that horse again. I'd never seen a finer animal, anywhere. Nice clean lines and built for travel.

In the cave, I built up my fire. There was nothing to eat for me, although the blue horse was doing all right judging by the sounds of cropping grass from the meadow. All that remained was for me to bed down. Picking up the saddle, I carried it well inside the cave.

A good saddle, a very good saddle, and some saddlebags. Come daylight I'd have a look at them. The Winchester was almost new, a '76, of .44 caliber. The saddle blanket was a Navajo.

The fire died down and I went to sleep, covering my shoulders with the saddle blanket. It was right chilly before daybreak but I stuck it out, trying to get all the sleep I could.

The cold awakened me, and I stirred the ashes to find a small bit of glowing wood, added some leaves and twigs until I got the fire going. By that time I was shivering and shaking. It took me a while to get settled down. When I'd warmed up I went down to the meadow and brought in the roan. He stood quiet whilst I saddled him up and slid my rifle into the sleeve.

The sky was overcast when I rode up out of the canyon and took a look-see around the country. Nothing was moving, so I rode on down to the trail and headed east. Where I was going I'd no idea, but what I wanted was distance. Looking back from time to time, I saw nothing, and that worried me more than had I seen a posse coming. You can run from a posse or fight it, but you can't run from what was worryin' me.

Mountains reared up on my left, set back from the trail but not far. The foothills were covered with aspen and scattered ponderosa pine, and a creek came down from the mountains, ran across in front of me, then headed west. The trail looked better. Wagon wheels had gone down this road and what looked like a stage.

Right now I was fetching up to be hungry. Not that missin' a meal or two was new to me, but I'd been hungry when I went for that drink and had planned to eat as soon as I'd washed down the dust from my throat. Now it had been more than two days and nights since I'd eaten and my stomach was beginning to think my throat had been cut.

Then we dipped down alongside the creek and up ahead I could see a big barn, some stacks of hay, and then a couple of other buildings, one of them a good-sized cabin. It was a house, sure enough, with an upstairs to it, and down at the barn there were horses in the corral and a couple of cows in another.

Loosening the Winchester in its scabbard and taking the thong from my six-shooter, I rode up to the house and stepped down from the saddle. Tying my horse in front of the granary or whatever it was, I walked up to the door and knocked.

Nothing happened. The latch string was not out and the door was strongly made. After a moment I rapped again and thought that time I heard movement inside. Then a woman's voice. "Who is it? What do you want?"

Well, what could I tell her? That I was a man escaping from a hanging?

"Sort of driftin', ma'am, and I ain't come by any grub lately. I was wonderin' if you could sort of let me set up an' put my feet under your table."

My eyes went to the gate. It was hanging loose, a top hinge busted. It had been a no-account hinge, anyway. Homemade it was, but made in the wrong home.

"Do you mean you are hungry?"

"That's one way of puttin' it, ma'am. Another would be to say I was starved."

The door opened. "Come in, please."

Taking off my hat, I ran my fingers through my hair. There was something in that voice . . . something I couldn't place.

Suddenly wary, I stepped through the door, pausing on the stoop to whip my hat against my pants to get rid of some of the dust, and taking time to give a quick glance around.

The house, what I could see of it, was spotlessly clean. There were curtains in the windows, and neatly made cushions on the chairs. The copper pots I could see shone like mirrors. Inside, everything was the exact opposite of what I'd seen outside, which looked to be a real rawhide sort of outfit. I'd seen a busted rail in the fence, and a lot that needed doin' outside.

She was at the fire, but at my step she turned to face me. She was taller than most women, with blond hair, quite a lot of it, tied in a neat bun at the back of her head.

"Please, please do come in. I—we do not often have visitors."

We? I looked around and saw nobody.

Awkward, because I suddenly realized I'd not shaved in a week and my hair needed combing. "I was just ridin' through, ma'am, and I've come a far piece an' my horse is wearied."

"Won't you be seated? You must have ridden far, for there are no ranches in some distance."

There was a wooden peg on the wall and I hung my hat, wishing again that I'd shaved.

She was beautiful, and there is something about a really beautiful woman that throws a man off. A pretty girl, now, she just warms a man up, but a really beautiful one is apt to make him tongue-tied and fixin' to run. This was such a woman. A golden blonde with only a slight wave in her hair, and features cut to classical perfection. Looked like one of them Greek statues, only not so full in the face.

There was sunlight in the room but shadows in her eyes, and shadows around them, too. "We do not have many visitors. I am glad you came by."

"I'd think every man in the country would be at your door," I said. "A body likes to look on a beautiful woman even if she belongs to somebody else."

"I belong to no one."

She spoke flat and cold, so I did not know how to respond. It just stopped me right where I was. It was not an invitation but a clear statement of fact, and left me with the impression she did not want anybody, either.

How could such a woman exist in such a place without a man? There was so much man's work to be done on this kind of outfit, and I'd seen enough tying up my horse to know it needed doing.

"Ma'am? I think I'd better tell you. There may be some men lookin' for me. If they come, I'll go out to meet them. No use you gettin' involved."

"A posse?"

"Yes, ma'am. I killed a man."

Her expression did not change. "So did I."

If she was interested in my reaction she offered no sign of it, but went to the stove and began dishing up something that smelled mighty good. It was stew, and she brought a heaping plate to the table. Taking up a fork, I started to eat, then stopped suddenly, looking at my food.

For the first time, she smiled. "I did not poison him."

"It wasn't that. I was waiting for you."

"Don't. I eat very little."

"It was a fair shooting," I said.

She offered no comment but filled two cups with coffee and placed one before me. She seated herself across the table and took her cup in both hands, looking across it at me.

"You said you were a drifter."

"I was working for an outfit in the Nation and decided to move west. I prospected some up around Hite."

"How did you find this place?"

"It wasn't me, it was my horse. You see, they'd taken me out to hang me, and when I got away there was only the horse they hung me from. They just sort of left it standin'. Well, I took out astraddle that horse an' that horse just naturally brung me here."

Her features tightened with shock. She clutched the edge of the table with both hands, her knuckles white. "Not . . . ? Not a blue roan?"

"Yes, ma'am, and a mighty fine—"

"My God!" she whispered. "Oh, my God!"

TWO

There was silence in the room with only the hiss of steam from the teakettle. A stick dropped in the potbellied stove.

"It was a shock. I thought that horse was gone, gone for good."

"He's a good horse, ma'am, a mighty fine horse, and he seemed to know where he was going."

"He was coming home."

"Yes, ma'am. Horses like their home. There's a few of them won't come home if given a chance, even if they've been treated bad."

She put down her cup. Her face was strained and her eyes had a haunted look. "You see, the man I killed was riding that horse."

"Sorry to bring bad memories. Ma'am, I'll ride him right out of here, if you want. Ride him so far you'll not see him again."

"He isn't my horse. He belongs to the lady who owns this place. To Mrs. Hollyrood."

"You're not the owner?"

For a moment there was bitterness in her expression. "I own nothing, I have nothing." She looked straight at me. "I was a drifter, too. She took me in, and I've tried to help."

"How many hands you got?"

"We're alone here. There was nobody on the ranch when we came, and Mrs. Hollyrood hired a cowboy. He used to be a soldier, a very hardworking man."

"He quit you?"

"He rode into town on Robin. That's the horse you are riding, and he was killed, shot down in a gunfight by a man named Houston Burrows." She looked straight into my eyes. "I believe he was deliberately tricked into a fight and killed. Mrs. Hollyrood does not believe it." She paused and then added, "For a woman who has been around as much as she has, she is quite naïve. She believes the best of everybody. That's her trouble."

"She hasn't had the ranch long, then?"

"Mrs. Hollyrood is an actress, and she has been an actress since she was a baby. Her parents were in a traveling company before the War and she with them. Mostly they played the South, and then the War came on. She married Mr. Hollyrood, and he enlisted in the Confederate cavalry. He rode with Jeb Stuart for a time and was killed at Gettysburg."

It was pleasant sitting there in the quiet kitchen, with sunlight coming through the windows. The kitchen was spotless.

"You'll need a couple of riders," I said, "and one should be handy with tools. I noticed a lot of fixin' up that needed doin'."

"I suppose you're right." She refilled our cups. "We've only been here a few weeks. You see, Mrs. Hollyrood inherited the ranch from an admirer, a Mr. Phillips."

"She was married to him?"

"No, they were just friends." She looked at me quickly. "And I don't mean lovers. Mr. Phillips was a lonely man and he saw something in her that appealed to him. They had dinner one night after a show and talked. After that he followed the show and they would meet and talk, go for long walks, and just spend time together. He told her if anything happened to him she would have the ranch.

"You know how those things are. Men, even the nicest of them, make promises simply because they want to be friendly, with no intention of deceiving, just making conversation. So she did not take him seriously. She was not a rancher and was not interested in ranching.

"They exchanged letters. It was company for her, too, and it can be lonely on the road. Then he was killed, gored by a steer, we heard. And he had done what he promised, left his ranch to her.

"The time was right. The company had fallen on bad times. There had been crop failures in some of the northern states and of course the South after the War was poverty-stricken. Our manager absconded with the money and we were all left with nothing.

"Well, almost nothing. Mrs. Hollyrood had saved a little and I'd managed to put by a few dollars, so we came out here."

She puzzled me, this young, lovely woman did. She looked fragile, yet I had an idea she was anything but that. She was almost too beautiful, the sort of beauty that can make a man uncomfortable.

"Did you say you were an actress, also?"

"Not a very good one. I'd been with the company only a few weeks when it closed, but Mrs. Hollyrood had been helpful and I had nowhere to go, so she suggested I come west with her."

The house was better built than most western houses which ranchers threw together hastily for shelter, and with little thought for comfort or convenience. That sort of thing came later, when they were established, and this country was new. The first settlers had just begun coming into the area ten years before, and the Utes weren't happy about it.

A door opened suddenly and a pretty, gray-haired woman came into the room. She had quick, intelligent eyes that took me in at a glance.

"I heard voices."

"Sorry, ma'am. Didn't mean to disturb you. I'm just passin' through." I'd gotten up in a hurry, my napkin in my left hand.

"Sit down, please. It isn't often we have visitors."

She seated herself at the head of the table and I sat down. The younger woman went to the stove for the coffeepot. "You're Passin' Through? What an interesting name!"

That made me smile, something I hadn't done much lately.

"It ain't exactly a name, ma'am. It's a condition. Now I find the horse I'm ridin' belongs to you."

"He's riding Robin," the girl said.

"Oh, no!" Shocked, she turned to me. "You mustn't, you know. He's a Death Horse. Even the Indians know it. Wherever he goes, somebody is killed."

"If folks want to get themselves killed there's no use blamin' the horse. That's a mighty fine animal, ma'am."

"Mr. Phillips told me about him before I ever came west. It started when they first threw him to brand. Two men disputed the ownership and fought over it. Both of them were killed, so one of the cowboys took a running iron and branded the colt with a death's-head, skull and crossbones.

"Almost a year later some Utes tried to steal him, and two of them were killed as well as a hand who tried to fight them off."

"Any other horses stolen?"

"A dozen, I believe."

"No death's-heads on them? They were there, too, ma'am. No use givin' the horse a bad name."

"Mr. Phillips said the Utes didn't like the brand and turned the horse loose. He came back, or started to. There was a man in town caught him up and rode him out here. I think he was sent to try to frighten us away. He was drinking heavily and he ordered us out of the house. We did not go, of course, and he threatened to burn us out.

"We ordered him off the place, but he swore at us, lit a torch, and started for the house, riding Robin. Matty shot him."

"I did not want to, but he was drunk and crazy. I was frightened."

"You did the right thing." I sipped coffee. "Any trouble with the law?"

"The sheriff came out, and that man was still lying there, the burned-out torch close to his hand. He was within six feet of the house."

The stew she had given me was finished so I refilled my cup. To tell the truth I didn't want to leave. I was a lone-riding man and this here was the first time I'd put my feet under a real table in a home since . . . well, since longer than I liked to recall.

"That riggin' belong to the dead man?"

"No, it belonged to McCarron, the hand we hired who was killed by Houston Burrows. Every time we try to hire anybody he frightens them off. After all, they have no loyalty to us. Not many men want to take a job when it means a fight."

"Seems like a lot of shootin' goin' on. Is it always like that?"

"Oh, no! There's very little, actually."

"You've a mighty fine place, ma'am. You're lucky to have it."

"It *is* nice. Mr. Phillips knew I'd been dreaming of a place of my own. You don't know what it's like on the road. You see, I knew nothing else from the time I was a small child, and I always dreamed of having a place of my own where I could just *stop*. Where I could grow things, belong to something."

"Well, you've got a place now. Handled right, you should make yourself a nice living."

"I'm afraid not, Mr. Passin'. We can't do the work by our-
selves. I can ride and so can Matty, but we just don't know
what to do."

Well, I shifted in my chair. I took up my cup, then put it
down. "Ma'am? If you'd like I could sort of stay on. I mean I
could stay for a while, get the place into shape for you."

"Oh? Would you? I think—!"

"Matty," Mrs. Hollyrood said, "you can't ask him to take the
risk. There's that awful Burrows man, and—"

"You don't need to worry about him," I said. "He'll not be
botherin' you no more."

"How can you be sure? He's a mean, cruel man, and he's
very dangerous."

"He might have been, ma'am, but he ain't dangerous no
more. I killed him."

You could have heard a leaf fall. There was a moment when
we heard a magpie scratchin' around outside, and the blue roan
stomped in the dust.

Mrs. Hollyrood was looking at me. "You said you *killed*
him?"

"Yes, ma'am. I was sort of passin' through town, an' stopped
for a drink and something to eat, and he picked trouble with
me. He was fixin' to kill me, ma'am, just because he wanted to
kill somebody. I was a stranger, just—"

" 'Passin' through'?"

"Yes'm. I was hot, tired, and hungry. All I wanted was a
quick drink, a meal, a bath, and a place to sleep. I wasn't
huntin' trouble but he was thinkin' himself a big, bad man and
just had to prove it."

"But you could have been killed!"

"Not by him, ma'am. Where I been, his kind are two for a
dollar. If they set in a corner an' keep quiet nobody pays 'em
much mind. He wouldn't make a pimple on a tough man's
neck. How big a man is depends on how big a territory he's
in."

I put down my cup. "Ma'am? If I'm to stay on I'd better get
busy. Comin' in I noticed the gate was busted, hangin' on one
hinge."

Getting up I said, "How many head of cattle you got, ma'am?
And how many horses?"

"I don't really know. Mr. Phillips kept accounts. If you like I
can—"

"Later, ma'am."

Outside the air was cool. I looked up and my eyes swept the long ridge, beginning in a sort of peak topped by ponderosa pine and ending in a rock that sort of stood off by itself, a fine sweep of country. Below the peak there was a forest of aspen. There was a big old barn and a granary opposite, and the road that led past the house disappeared down the valley. It was a good piece of country of which I knew nothing at all.

Matty came to the door. "It's late. McCarron slept in the granary there. I see you have no bedding, and—"

"I'll make do, ma'am. I been doin' it all my life."

"There will be breakfast in the morning. Please come when you get up."

That made me smile. "Ma'am, I never slept past daylight in my life, and mostly I'm up long before."

"Come when you're ready," she repeated, "breakfast will be ready."

Stripping the gear off the roan, I turned him into the corral and put out some hay for him and a bait of corn in a bucket. Whilst he was eating I curried him some. He was a good horse and he'd carried me far and fast.

Currying that horse gave me time to consider. It looked to me like Mrs. Hollyrood and Matty were in a peck of trouble. Seemed like somebody wanted them off this place, but maybe I was jumping the gun. Maybe it was just happenstance that McCarron got himself killed and that other man threatened to burn them out.

Houston Burrows had picked a fight with McCarron and killed him, but maybe it was simply that Burrows was a trouble hunter. There was one in every town, and it was usually strangers they picked on, strangers or somebody they knew they could handle. The trouble with a stranger is that you never know who you've challenged, and there were all kinds of men driftin' western country, men like Chris Madsen, the Oklahoma marshal, who had served his time in the French Foreign Legion before coming to America.

There was a lantern hangin' inside the door of what was called the granary and I lit it and looked around. There was half of the place given over to sacks of oats and a bin of unshelled corn on one side, and beyond a partition there was a bunk, a chair, and a small table with a washstand. The bunk was made up army-style, a clean white sheet and a blanket drawn tight and tucked in. Some clothes hung on the wall on homemade hangers and the floor was swept. This would be a tough act to follow.

There was a tub made from a barrel sawed in half. I'd seen it standing in the granary side so I got it out, filled it half-full with water, and bathed. Believe me, it felt mighty good after the long ride I'd been on. Meanwhile I thought of my two horses and gear left behind when I left town after bein' hung. Nobody had seen me leave them, and they'd hold the horses for a while and might not even find my gear, yet I'd no wish to go back and risk hangin'.

The bed felt good, but tired as I was I could have slept on a bed of logs. The morning was gray before my eyes opened and I crawled out of bed, dressed, then made the bed as carefully as I'd found it.

There was light from the kitchen, but first off I took a careful look around. The big old barn loomed dark and ominous. Come daylight I'd walk over and give it some attention. The blue roan walked over to the fence when I came by and I leaned on the top bar and talked to him.

"We both got a bad name," I spoke softly, scratching his neck, "only I earned mine, an' you just happened to be around. When we leave here we'll go together, you an' me."

Turning toward the house, I stopped and put my hand up to my jaw. Three days' growth of beard . . . I walked back inside and shaved into the rectangle of mirror held against the door-post by four nails. Only then did I cross to the house.

The door opened at once. "You're late," Matty said.

"I had to go back and shave." My fingers went to my jaw. "Out in the hills a man can forget."

"You shouldn't." Her look was cool, appraising. "You're a good-looking man."

Me? I was astonished, and embarrassed. Somehow I'd never thought of my looks, one way or the other.

THREE

It was warm and comfortable in the kitchen. Crossing to a chair at the table, I put my hat on the floor close at hand. There were two coal-oil lamps on the walls with reflectors behind them, and there was a glow from the kitchen range.

"Do you like oatmeal, Mr. Passin'?"

"I do, ma'am, and bacon, too." I had seen her slicing it into the frying pan.

She was busy at the stove, then dished up the oatmeal for me. "We have a cow," she added, "a milk cow."

Milk cows weren't common in range country, but this here was different, being a mixed lot of country. They ran cattle here, and higher in the mountains, sheep. Mostly it was mining country.

"My name isn't Passin' Through," I said, "that was Mrs. Hollyrood's joke."

"You did not tell us your name, and one of the things we have learned out here is not to ask a man's name or where he is from," Matty said. "To us you are Mr. Passin' until you decide to tell us something else."

Well, I didn't know her name, either, when it came to that, and I was not asking questions. Besides, what does a name mean? Nothing, until a man makes it mean something.

The oatmeal was good but I was taking my time. It had been a long time since I'd set down in such a pleasant place to eat, and served up by such a woman. Come to that, I'd never known anyone like her, nor anyone near as beautiful. When it comes to asking questions, she was not the sort you'd ask.

"That posse hasn't appeared."

"No, ma'am, an' I'm not real anxious they should."

17

"Will you run?"

Now I didn't like the sound of that. No man wants a woman to think he'd run, and when it came to that, I'd run as far as I intended to go.

"No, ma'am. If I see 'em in time I'll go hole up in the hills yonder. I wouldn't want to have no lead flyin' around you womenfolks."

"These walls are thick. They are squared logs, Mr. Passin', and if a person were to stay away from windows there would not be too much to worry about."

She brought the bacon to the table, then sat down opposite me. "We have no eggs but Mrs. Hollyrood plans to raise chickens. We will have some soon."

"Yes, ma'am. It's been almost a year since I had eggs. That was out in Pioche, Nevada."

"Pioche? I've heard of it. A rough town, they say."

"Sort of. There was shootin', time to time. They say they buried seventy-five men before one died of sickness. They seemed right proud of that fact. I've heard of places where the climate was so healthy they had to shoot somebody so's they could start a graveyard, but those folks in Pioche sort of over-did it."

"Are you a miner, Mr. Passin'?"

"I'm anything it takes to get the coon. When there's mines, I work at minin', and when there's cows, that's my game. A man has to adjust."

"And if there's shooting?"

"That's part of the adjustin'. I was brought up to respect the rights of others and to protect my own self and my rights. Out in this rough country when it's new, there isn't any law standin' around to protect folks. You got to do it yourself and the law expects it of you. There'd be mighty few marshals or sheriffs around if they had to do all the shootin' themselves. Some of us folks have to sort of trim around the edges, like."

"I understand." She looked like she did, too. And she'd shot that man chargin' the house with a torch. This here was a woman a man would have to treat gentle. Not that I'd treat one any other way, if I had one. And that was unlikely, me bein' a driftin' man with no fixed abode and mighty little silver showin'. She puzzled me some.

The fire crackled, and she got up, lifted a lid on the stove, and added a chunk of pine. I finished the oatmeal and moved closer to the bacon. She filled my cup.

"Where I come from," I said, "we weren't Sunday shooters. I mean we weren't folks who went out of a Sunday to shoot at targets. We boys had to hunt meat for the table or we didn't eat. My pa, he was away workin'. He'd no time to hunt so it fell to me. He'd give me six balls and the powder for them, and come evenin' I had to have six pieces of game, the unfired balls, or a da—a mighty good explanation as to why I missed. I didn't miss much."

"I know," Matty said quietly, "it was the same with us."

"Your brothers?"

"With me. I did the hunting until I was twelve, then my mother died and my father took me away from all that. He went back to riding the boats."

Well, I looked at her. "The riverboats?"

"My father was a gambling man. He'd quit when he married my mother, but when she died he went back to it and took me along."

Those riverboat gamblers were a smooth lot. They were gentlemen, mostly, men who had been southern planters who lost it all during the War. Or there were some who posed as southern gentlemen but were not. Gambling on the riverboats needed a smooth hand.

"He was a wonderful man," Matty said, "and I loved him very much. He sent me away to school and I did well but never liked it. I liked being on the boats with him, and in the summer, I was."

"What happened?"

"He made a big winning one night, very big. I was sixteen then, and he had always told me that when he made his stake we would go back to Boston, that was where he came from, and live there.

"There were some gamblers on board who worked together. My father outwitted them and won and they came after him. He never got back to our stateroom."

"Murdered?"

"Yes." She was quiet for a moment and then she said, "He was stabbed as he was passing the stacks of firewood when he was coming back to our cabin. They robbed him and threw his body overboard. I heard the splash."

Her face was pale, her eyes large in the lamplight. "Tough,"

I said, "sixteen and alone on a riverboat. Did you have any money at all?"

She looked at me, her face very still, very cool. "I had it all," she said. "I had everything he'd won."

"But—!"

"I was up, waiting for him to come in. I heard him fall, a moment of scuffling, and then the splash. They went to their cabin, and when I opened the door one of them was wiping off a bloody knife. If the blow had not killed him the knife would."

"You *followed* them?"

"I did. And I told them I wanted my money. They laughed at me and I shot one of them through the ear. There were three of them in the room and my father's money was on the table. I told them to put it into the pillowcase and give it to me. 'Next time,' I said, 'it won't be just an ear.' "

Well, I just looked at her, and you know something? I believed her. She could have done it.

"That was rough going for sixteen years old," I commented.

"Where I come from sixteen years is grown-up, and my father had taught me that someday I'd be on my own. I'd no choice. A sixteen-year-old girl left alone on a steamboat with almost no money?"

She looked at me over her cup. "That was four years ago. I took some of the money and went back to school. I needed the education but I also needed time to think, to decide what to do.

"It was a fashionable school, and the girls lived well, so I did, too. Then some of us slipped out one night to see Mrs. Hollyrood's company perform. Traveling shows were not considered very nice. They were not 'respectable,' so they were forbidden. But we went, I saw the show and thought it was fun. I went to Mrs. Hollyrood and asked for a job. They needed a girl, so I left school and went with them."

Mrs. Hollyrood appeared in her bedroom door. She was wearing a Japanese kimono. "Some men are coming. I am afraid we are in trouble!

"There are five of them," she added, "and they look rough."

FOUR

Standing well back from the window, I watched them ride down the lane and up to the house. One face looked familiar and as I watched I remembered. He was the one who put the noose around my neck.

Mrs. Hollyrood went to the door. "How do you do? Is there something I can do for you gentlemen?"

"You can move out," one of them said. He was slim, wiry, and wore his gun butt forward on the left side. A man wearing a gun in that position can draw with either hand. At least two of the riders with him had been drinking. "I don't know what kind of a trick you used on my uncle, but this here ranch belongs to me."

"I am afraid you are mistaken." She had dignity and she was cool. "The arrangement was all perfectly legal, and Mr. Phillips had the papers drawn up and witnessed."

"That's no account. This here place is mine. I'm his legal heir and I want you off of it. I want you off now."

She smiled. I could see that from where I stood. "I am sorry, gentlemen, I like it here and have no intention of leaving. The ranch is mine. If necessary I can call the sheriff."

"To do that you got to ride into town. Do you think you'll make it?"

She smiled again, very sweetly. "It has been my understanding," she said, "that western men treated ladies with consideration. Am I to understand that you are threatening me?"

One of the other riders, an older man with a beard, muttered something, but the wiry one shook his head. "Threatenin'? No, it's just a warnin'. This here's a rough time, lots of Injuns ridin' who don't care who they shoot."

21

Suddenly one of the riders noticed the blue roan.

"Lew? What's that roan doin' here?"

The wiry one addressed as Lew turned irritably, then saw the horse. He turned back to Mrs. Hollyrood. "Where'd that roan come from? How'd he get here?"

"This is his home. If you are related to Mr. Phillips you should know that. He belongs here."

"That's a bad-luck horse, Lew. I don't want nothin' to do with it."

"He won't be bad luck anymore," Lew said suddenly. "I'll shoot him."

Stepping past Mrs. Hollyrood, I said, "Leave that horse alone. I like him."

They were shocked. They had no idea there was anyone else about, although they might have known of Matty.

"Who the hell—?"

"Hey!" The man who put the noose around my neck recognized me. "Ain't you—?"

"I am. I'm the man you hung. It didn't seem to take, somehow."

Nobody said anything. They simply stared, and the man who put the noose around my neck swallowed a couple of times and looked like he would like to be somewhere else, anywhere else. It is one thing to put a rope around a man's neck when you're backed by a crowd and he's alone. It is quite something else when you are facing that man, just thirty feet away, and he is armed.

The man called Lew slowly moved his hand away from his gun. "You the one who killed Houston Burrows? He was a good man with a gun."

"Not where I come from."

Again there was silence. One of the men who showed signs of drinking now looked cold sober. He backed his horse a few steps. "It's gettin' late," he suggested.

Lew didn't like the situation. He looked like he wanted to do something or say something to save face, but everything that came to mind was provocative.

He wanted to get off the hook and I just didn't give a damn. He'd come to drive two women off a ranch that rightfully belonged to one of them, and I just didn't care what he did, but if he did the wrong thing he'd be bedded down in Boot Hill tomorrow.

There were four of them and one of me but I knew what I could do and what I had to do. Two of them were ready to run at the first move and the third hadn't made up his mind.

The one I was going to kill first wasn't the one who put the noose around my neck. It was a square-built gent with a bullet head who sat a bay horse just to the right of Lew. I didn't know his name but he was the tough one.

I gave them a minute to worry themselves and then said, "Why don't you boys just ride out of here? The gate's open, but be damned sure you close it when you leave."

Two of them already had their horses moving before I stopped talking.

Lew, he sat there a minute. He was stubborn and thought well of himself. When he told about this in town, he wanted the story to make him look good.

"I'm goin', but we'll be seein' you again."

"Why wait?" I went down the stone steps to the road. "I'm here right now, and maybe Houston Burrows is wantin' comp'ny."

Lew didn't like it. He backed off and turned his horse. "A man talkin' like that can get hisself killed."

"Maybe, but I won't go alone. I'll have a couple of dogs to lay at my feet."

They walked their horses away and did not look back. I stood in the center of the road watching them go, but I wasn't even thinking of them. I was thinking of my two horses in that faraway town and my outfit. If I figured on prospecting I was going to need what I had, if somebody hadn't already gone south with it.

When I went back in the house they had filled my cup again so I sat down. Mrs. Hollyrood looked across her cup at me. "Mr. Passin', you're a brave man."

"No, ma'am. Just a man. A man who's spent his life ridin' rough country, an' I just don't know no better."

"Thank you. I don't know what I would have done."

"Yes, you do." I looked across the table at her. "You'd have done what I did, only maybe different." I looked over at Matty standing beside the kitchen range. "And she knew what she would do."

Matty didn't say anything nor turn her head to look at me. That woman . . . well, there was something about her.

*   *   *

Anyplace like that where there hasn't been a man around keepin' things up will slip into decline. This one had just gotten started, so I went around repairin' a fence rail here, cleanin' stalls there, just generally keepin' myself busy. Also, I kept an eye on the road and on the low hill back of the house.

There were some fine meadows that would grow a good stand of grass, and I could see where cattle had been feeding under the scrub-oak trees, and bedding down there, too. Later that day I took a ride along the edge of one of the meadows. There were deer tracks, and near a small pool I saw a bear track.

The country I was riding was higher than the house, and both the house and the road leading past it were clearly visible. The dim game trail I followed led through the scrub oak and along the slope below the ridge. I rode east, constantly looking off toward the La Platas, bulking against the sky to the north. There was a good deal of down timber, as there nearly always is in wild country. A man could make a few trips with a wagon and bring back wood enough for the coming winter. Dipping down, the trail led into the aspen below the highest peak.

It was very still, there was no sound but the hoof falls of the blue roan. The horse walked, ears pricked, into the stillness of the forest. Finally, we reached the edge where I could see along the trail toward the east. To the north, up La Plata Canyon, lay Parrott City, a town that had come into being a few years back to supply miners working silver deposits in the La Platas. Further west there were a couple of other towns.

The place where my horses and gear had been left was off to the northwest and a good long ride away. Somewhere east there was a place called Animas City, but I'd never been there. This was new country for me.

Here and there I saw cattle, and when I figure to judge the worth of land for grazing I just look at the stock. These cattle were fat and lazy, so they were getting plenty to eat without rustling too much for it. Again I saw bear tracks and some droppings.

Looking across the country toward the La Platas, I could see where a creek came down, cutting diagonally across the mountainside. That would be Starvation Creek, named by some men

who came into the country with John Moss, who founded
Parrott City.

Turning the roan, I walked him back through the woods to
the other side where I could see back along the trail toward the
house. Nothing moved back there.

My eyes followed the ridge to the rocky promontory that
stood out over the green valley to the west of it. I'd have to
ride that ridge and see what lay on the other side. Meanwhile I
was doing some serious thinking.

What would Lew and his outfit do now? That he wanted the
ranch was obvious, but as things stood he had no clear claim to
it. Still, if he could run Mrs. Hollyrood off he might be able to
establish a claim on the abandoned place as next of kin. Most of
us knew a little about the law from setting in on trials and
suchlike, but that was an area of which I knew nothing.

In the smaller towns throughout the country, trial lawyers
were like stars in the theater. When court was setting, folks
would drive or ride in from miles around just to see the show,
and the trial lawyers played to us in the gallery as much as to
the jury, and some of the more flamboyant lawyers had follow-
ings who bragged them up and told story after story about what
they said or who they quoted.

Most of the lawyers had read from the Bible and the classics
and they could quote freely, and did. Some of them had a story
for every occasion, and a story would often make a point when
nothing else would.

Folks would come in from miles around like to a revival
meeting and they would bring picnic lunches. Wagons, buckboards, surreys, and horses would be tied around the court
house whilst the owners were inside listening to the trials.
Some lawyers drew packed houses, and often the cases were
decided on common sense rather than any point of law.

A man quoting the Bible had to be almighty sure of himself
because most folks read the Bible and heard it quoted every
Sunday and considerable on weekdays. Church wasn't a place
where folks went only for religious reasons. It was a social
occasion, a chance to meet the people who lived around the
country, and if a man expected to do business, that was where
he would meet the outstanding men of the community. All the
young sprouts went because that was also a place to meet girls,
and many a wedding developed from flirtations begun at church
or one of the church socials they were always having.

Many a man who had small interest in religion as such could quote from the Bible because of what he had heard in church.

Mine was a churchgoing family, and to get to church from where I was raised we had to get up before daylight, and ride in an old spring wagon over ten miles of rough road, or at least a trail we called a road but which nobody from anywhere else would have recognized as such.

My thoughts turned back to Matty. I'd heard no other name for her, and folks in our country just didn't ask for names. You took what was handed to you or you started callin' somebody "Shorty" or "Slim" or "Red" or whatever. Sometimes a man would give you his handle and you'd use it, calling him whatever he said.

Matty was a strange woman. My guess was that she was about twenty years old. Most were married by that time. She was a downright beautiful woman but she didn't act like she wanted you to notice. Her face was still, with only her eyes busy. Come to think of it, had I ever seen her smile? I could not remember.

Mrs. Hollyrood, on the other hand, was one who smiled a lot. She was a pleasant, attractive woman.

When I got back to the ranch I stripped the gear from the roan and turned him into the corral, pitching some hay to him. Then I went to the granary, which doubled as a bunkhouse, and I washed up. There was a shelf outside the door and a towel hung there, with a washbasin and soap. The water was cold, but I could remember only a few times in my life when I'd washed up in warm water.

Drying my hands, I stood close to the log wall and studied the country back of the house, then down the valley where the road went, getting to know the trees and clumps of brush so any change would show up right away. It was second nature for a man like me to be careful.

A lot of what a man sees is sort of instinct, I guess. You notice how the shadows fall, and if there's a thicker shadow than should be, or a shadow where none had been before, you take care.

Sooner or later, scouting around like I'd been doing, I would locate all the good spots which a hidden marksman might use for cover. Then I could keep an eye on them. It was not difficult to select the danger spots. Anybody figurin' on dry-gulching somebody picks a spot where he can be hidden and which offers some shelter from return fire, as well as an easy escape route. He will try to choose a place where he just naturally fits into the scenery.

Mrs. Hollyrood was at the table when I knocked on the door. She looked mighty pleasant settin' there, her hair all done just so. She always looked as if she'd stepped out of a bandbox, neat as a pin and comfortable as a cat.

"Mr. Passin'! How nice! Won't you come in and sit down? Will you have some coffee?"

"Yes, ma'am, I surely would."

"You've been riding?"

"Scoutin' the country, sort of. You got any idea how much stock you've got, ma'am?"

"There is an account book. Mr. Phillips said I'd find it all there. I'll get it if you wish."

"Tomorrow." Seated at the table, I looked around. Women-folks had a way of makin' things nice. Me, I'd lived in bunk-houses or just out in the country so long this here seemed like sheer luxury. It was easy to see how a man could get himself married—

Shocked, I gulped coffee and burned myself. A man could get himself into trouble with thoughts like that.

"Mr. Passin'? I wonder if you would consider working for me?"

Well, I looked at her. I'd never seen a more pleasant-lookin' woman. "No, ma'am," I said, "I wouldn't."

FIVE

She was expectin' a different sort of answer, and maybe my reply was kind of abrupt, so I said, "I had my fill of workin' for folks. Enjoyed it now and again, but I've a notion to just wander off in wild country and live best as I can."

"That could be a lonely life."

"Yes, ma'am. I been lonely most of what's behind me, so I'm used to it." I paused a moment. "I'll stay on here an' sort of get things fixed up an' straightened out, an' I don't want money. I cleaned up a pocket out yonder that left me with a mite to go on."

The coffee wasn't quite so hot when I tried it again. "This place needs some fixin' an' it goes against my nature to see a fine place get run down. Besides"—I smiled at her—"a little home cookin' goes mighty good. I never was much hand in a kitchen, an' when on the trail I just eat along the way. Jerky and the like of what I can find whilst travelin'. Sometimes I go days without a proper meal."

"Do you have a trade?"

"Not so's you'd notice. I punched cows here an' there, drove a freight wagon, guided hunters goin' into the mountains after bear an' such, an' I've trapped a mite, and was marshal of a minin' town over in Nevada, rode shotgun on a stage. I do whatever will get the coon, ma'am."

"Have you ever been married?"

"No, ma'am. Womenfolks don't cotton to me too much. I'm a rough man with rough ways. Anyway, womenfolks have to find a man with roots, a man who belongs somewhere or to something. She's got to take into account she may have a child and she's got to have a roof over her head and a place to raise him.

28

A woman's generally lookin' for a man with cattle on the hills or goods on the shelf, and well she should be. I'm a driftin' man, ma'am."

She smiled. "Just passin' through?"

"Yes, ma'am. That's mostly what I been doin' since I was knee-high to a short frog. I just want to be let alone." I paused, then looked up at her. "That gent I killed back yonder? He was pressin' for trouble. He felt himself a big man an' couldn't see how short was the shadow he cast. All I wanted was one drink, a meal, an' a chance to sleep under a roof again."

"You felt no remorse?"

"No, ma'am, he got what he wanted to give me. When a man goes huntin' trouble, or stealin' other folks' property, he's got to realize there's some won't stand for it. He depends on a threat to your life to take what's yours, whether it's your property or just your peace of mind.

"Ridin' alone, a man gets time to think. This here civilization we got is a mighty flimsy thing. There's laws, of course, but there's also an unspoken agreement among folks to abide by the rights of others. Anybody can make a mistake, but if he continues makin' that mistake he's shown himself unwilling to abide by the customs of others and so has no place in civilization.

"There was a time when ever'body was robbin' an' raidin' like them Vikings, but times changed and some folks never have realized it. They are mostly cases of what the Earl called arrested development."

"The 'Earl'?"

"He was an Englishman who hired me for a guide. He wanted to hunt but mostly he wanted to see the country. He killed a grizzly, some mountain goats, and other game. In camp he spent most of his time with books, readin', takin' down notes. I think he figured on writin' a book or some such thing. We used to talk around the campfire of an evenin'.

"That man I killed? If I hadn't stopped him then he'd probably have killed a half-dozen before somebody bedded him down on Boot Hill. He took me for some driftin' cowpuncher, but that's the trouble. When you take a hand in the gun game, you never know what the other man's holdin'."

We talked on, of the ranch, of her shows, of the home she always wished for, but she did not talk of Matty, whom I was curious about. Not that I had any business bein' curious.

The shadows came from the trees and crept into the folds of

the hills. Matty came down from her room upstairs and commenced getting supper on. It was mighty lazylike an' warm and I surely liked it, although it made me nervous, too, because just when a man gets settled down to comfort is when he forgets to expect trouble. Getting up, I went out the side door, which was in the shadows and had no light inside. Walking alongside the house, I stood listening into the night. It was cool as it always is of a night in the mountains or desert.

It was almighty quiet, and the stars were like distant campfires on the plain of night. The road lay white and empty and I could hear the horses down at the corral, but no other sound. Nevertheless, I didn't like it. That Lew struck me as a mean, vicious man and not one to stand by and lose something he thought he should have.

Nor was I sure those who had tried to hang me had given up. That town was a good distance back along the trail, but some of them ranched down this way and might be around anywhere. I'd know some of them by sight, but not all. It made me wonder about my goods back there. Had my pack been found? And what of my horses? They weren't so much but that was all I had.

Coming down here I'd traveled fast, most of the way. Going back it would take twice as long, maybe more.

The trees were black against the hillside. I looked along the road again. This was a much-traveled road and the house had once been a stage station. Anybody might be riding by, and I couldn't get jumpy at every sound.

When I came in and closed the door Matty glanced my way. "I was about to call you. Supper's ready."

She glanced at my gun. "Do you always wear that?"

"Yes, ma'am. My pa went to the fields one day. He was plowin' in the north forty, figurin' to put in a crop of corn. He'd worn a gun a good bit but figured it would be in the way and he left it hangin' on a nail inside the door.

"That was nearin' the end of the War, and some guerrillas come by wanted Pa's horses, so they shot him down and took our horses."

"Mightn't they have killed him anyway?"

"Yes, ma'am. Pa wasn't all that good with a gun. They might have, but they might not have even tried, seein' him armed. They might have just ridden on an' stole horses they could take without trouble.

"Even if they'd taken his, he could've made a fight. Why should he turn belly up an' scared just because some tinhorn thief wants what he has? If a man goes down fightin', that's one thing; if he's killed without a chance, that's somethin' else."

"You were left alone?"

"Yes, ma'am. Neighbor folks, they come over an' helped bury Pa. They wished for me to come live with them but they had all they could do to feed the ones they had, so I stayed on the place."

"Alone?"

"No, ma'am. I had Pa's Remington, some chickens, an' we had pigs runnin' in the woods. We had some hams and bacon sides in the smokehouse, and I stayed on, fixin' for myself. I swapped Pa's plow for a horse and the use of a harrow. We had seed corn so I planted that field my own self, just as I'd been helpin' Pa.

"The War ended an' folks began comin' home, and one day I was down to town and I saw a big feller in a checkered shirt. He'd been one of the guerrillas who killed Pa. He come into the store whilst I was there, and there were other folks around, so I spoke up, right to his face.

"I kep' my voice low but loud enough so's folks could hear and I said, 'You're the man murdered my pa.'

"Well, ma'am, that store got almighty still. He stared at me, tryin' to scare me. I was only ten years old but I didn't scare much.

" 'You're crazy, boy. I've never been in this country before.' He was wearin' a gun and most folks in the store were not.

" 'I'm not crazy,' I said, 'an' that horse you rode into town was Pa's. Now he's mine.'

"Ever'body was starin' at him an' he didn't like it. He stared hard at me but I stared right back. 'Pa was plowin',' I said, 'you rode up an' shot him down. Him unarmed an' helpless, then you taken his horses. You're a thief, mister, a damn thief an' a murderer.'

" 'If you was a man you wouldn't say that. As it is I've a good mind to—'

" 'I wouldn't think of it, was I you,' the storekeeper was speakin'. 'The boy's right. I remember that horse.'

" 'So do I,' another said. 'Mister, you better leave town whilst you're able. An' leave afoot. If you try to ride that horse you'll never make it.'

"Well, ma'am, he looked around. There was five or six people in the store, womenfolks as well as men, and he couldn't kill 'em all, and there were folks in the street.

" 'You're wrong,' he says, 'the boy's lyin'.'

"He put his hand on the door and backed out, but as he went out the door he said, 'I'll be seein' you!'

"The town had no marshal. The sheriff was forty miles away at the county seat an' there wasn't much anybody could do, but that man in the checkered shirt didn't know that. He left town an' he left my horse behind.

"Folks walked out on the boardwalk in front of the store and they called out to men across the street, and that feller, he just left out of there. He stole a horse on the edge of town and was gone."

"You never saw him again?"

"Yes, ma'am. I was sixteen when I saw him next. He was cuttin' a wide swath out west, makin' like a big, bad man. I was man grown an' wearin' a gun, and it was in the Territory. He was havin' a drink in a jug saloon, one of them where when you asked for a drink they poured it from a jug settin' under the counter.

"He was makin' himself big in front of folks, some of them Indians who lived there, some driftin' riders, an' what all.

" 'You got a big mouth,' I said.

"He turned to look at me, peerin' at me from under heavy eyebrows. 'Ain't I seen you before?'

" 'Twice,' I told him, 'once when you murdered my pa, and him unarmed and workin' in the field, an' another time when I was ten years old an' made you give up the horse you stole off my pa.'

"His face turned red and he began to sweat. All those brags he'd been makin' were starin' him in the face and those tough Territory boys were lookin' to see what he'd do.

" 'You ain't ten now,' he threatened.

" 'That's right. I'm man grown an' wearin' a gun, so you've got it to do.'

"Well, the sweat was standin' out on his forehead, and if ever I saw yellow in a man it was showin' up in him, but all I could think of was Pa, workin' hard to support a family on a two-by-twice farm, an' this man comin' along and murderin' him for his horse. Pa, who never did harm to any man.

"He looked around like he wanted a way out, but there wasn't any. Folks had drawed back, leaving him standin' alone.

"Sweat was drippin' off his nose and chin although it wasn't warm in there. All the nerve had gone out of him, and suddenly I didn't want to kill him no more. He was dead already, inside.

"This was our fight an' nobody was puttin' their two cents in. It was like that in the Territory, them days. You did what you had to do an' folks left it to you. You went to robbin' an' killin' outside of the Territory and those marshals would surely come huntin' you, but down there nobody cared very much.

" 'If there's a hell,' I said, 'there's a special place waitin' for you.'

"He just stood there, lookin' suddenly gaunt an' empty, so I started for the door. It had not been a pretty sight and I wanted to get out of there. I'd taken two steps before I heard somebody gasp, an' I swear I heard his gun clearin' leather. Turning, I saw his gun comin' level and I shot him in the brisket. His gun went off, the bullet strikin' over the door, but he was cold dead an' fallin'."

Matty put the supper on, and called Mrs. Hollyrood. She turned and looked straight at me in a way she had. "Why did you tell me that story?"

"I don't know. Never told anybody before. Maybe I wanted you to see I'm not a very nice man."

"Sit down," she said, "don't wait for her. She will be along."

Outside I could hear the clop-clop of horses' hoofs and the creak of a buckboard, but whoever it was did not stop, although it was a long way to Animas City.

Mrs. Hollyrood came out and the two of them talked about the place and about a copy of *Scribner's* and the ads in it.

There was a guitar standin' in the corner and I was wishful for music but said nothing. It was time I was gettin' on down the road, and as soon as I'd branded some stock and fixed things up, I'd start. I did want my outfit, though, wanted it the worst way.

"Mr. Phillips," Mrs. Hollyrood said, "had many copies of magazines. If you wish anything to read—"

"I'm not much of a reader," I said, ashamed. "I never had much schoolin'."

"But you can read, can't you?"

"A mite, ma'am." I pushed back from the table. "I'm gettin'
up early. I better hit the hay."

I started for the door, then thought of what I was doing and
went to the side door which opened on darkness and in darkness. I stepped outside. Standin' there I swore softly, bitterly.

Out in the desert or mountains I was all right, but I surely
wasn't much account with folks. To tell the truth, I wasn't
much of a hand when it come to readin'. Given time I could
sort of figure out the words, but I never read in front of folks
where they could see me workin' at it.

Seemed like much as I was wishful of readin' I was mostly
out on the range or somewhere and books weren't handy.
Tracks on a trail were easy for me, and I could read brands, but
a newspaper or a book was troublesome.

These were good women, real nice, and I wanted to help,
but then I'd best move along down the road. Meanwhile I'd
better fight shy of them as much as could be. The mud of
human affection could get pretty deep around here and I
wasn't of a mind to get myself stuck in it.

The road was white through the blackness. Waiting, I listened. No sound, and then—

Something stirred down there, something moved against the
white, then vanished. My hand was close to my gun and I
slipped the thong from the hammer.

Where I stood was blackness, but to get to the bunkhouse in
the granary I had to cross that white road, and I had a hunch
somebody was waitin', just down the trail.

They were stirring about inside, then the light in the kitchen
was blown out.

A boot grated on gravel—

Leaning my shoulder against the corner of the house, I put
my right hand on my gun. It was a poor light for shootin' but
I'd done it before.

SIX

There was vague light from the bedroom windows upstairs, for the windows were curtained. A soft wind moved a dried leaf across the gravel of the road, and the aspen leaves brushed their pale palms. Somebody or something was out there in the night, something as watchful as I, something waiting.

Waiting for me to move? Waiting to kill me? Or some passing traveler wondering if he should ask for shelter from the already darkened house?

Did he know that only women lived here? Or did he know about me? Was he looking for me?

The wind stirred again, rustling the leaves, and I waited. No sign of a horse. Was he afoot or did he leave his horse back up the road? Or did he hope to steal a horse here?

An Indian? This was Ute country and folks were saying the Utes were mighty unhappy about a lot of things. I knew the Utes. They were tough people, good fighting men and not about to be pushed around by anyone. If they went on the warpath it would mean a lot of good people were going to get hurt.

Yonder in the granary I had a good bed waiting, and I was tired, ready to turn in. My eyes searched the shadows. What I had heard sounded like a boot on gravel, and that meant whoever was out there was not likely to be an Indian.

What this place needed was a good dog, a watchdog who would make himself known. There should be one on the place before I left. A dog right now would know that man was out there and would tell us when people arrived or left.

As for myself I understood my position. If somehow I was shot, nobody would pay much attention. I was a drifter whom nobody knew and about whom nobody cared. My death would be a matter of conversation for a few hours or days depending on what else there was to talk about.

Things had quieted down inside with all the lights out and I believed the womenfolks had gone to bed. My eyes were accustomed to the darkness now and I could make things out pretty good.

Whoever was out there could not know I was outside. He might have seen me go in, he might have seen me through the windows, although I doubted it. I believed he arrived just as I was coming out and when I first heard him. I did not know that, however. Yet, the chances were he believed all here were inside and in bed. Leaning against the corner of the house, I waited while the slow minutes passed. Suddenly the roan blew loudly, and I could see his head was up and he was listening, watching something.

A shadow detached itself from the other shadows and a man stood in the road looking toward the house.

"Whatever you've got in mind," I said, "you'd better forget it. We don't take kindly to prowlers."

He stood very still. He was in the open and I was in deep shadow. He was wearing a narrow-brimmed hat and a suit.

"I'm looking for a woman," he said.

"You can prob'ly find one at Parrott City. Just ride west three or four miles an' take the canyon road. It's up the road a piece."

"I don't mean that kind of woman. It is very important that I find her."

"You usually do your lookin' at night? Prowlin' in the dark? A man got himself killed a while back. He fell not ten feet from where you stand. If it was daylight you might see the blood."

"I heard of that." He didn't seem fazed by it, not one bit. This was a cool character. He kept his voice even and low, just as I did, and he hadn't tried to move an inch.

"My advice is to move on down the trail. We got nothing for you here."

"I have it now. You're the man who killed Burrows!"

When I did not reply he shifted his feet, the first move he'd made since I first spoke. "Burrows was said to be quick."

"He thought so."

"You could help me. There'd be fifty dollars in it."

"I've got fifty dollars."

"I've heard there was a woman here, living on this ranch. I want to talk to her."

"Come in the daytime. There's womenfolks on several ranches around here. They're friendly folks, most of them. But they don't take to prowlers."

"I'm not a prowler. I was traveling late."

"We've talked enough. You'd better hit the trail."

"The woman who owns this place? She is a young woman?"

"She's a handsome woman. A lady. I make it a practice never to guess a woman's age. She has beautiful gray hair, if that helps."

"*Gray?*" His disappointment was obvious.

"You'd better move," I said. "It's past my bedtime. If you have any idea of comin' back, come in the daytime."

"The woman I'm looking for is young—"

"Mister, I don't give a damn who you're lookin' for. I just run out of patience. You light a shuck."

"I'm going. The woman I'm looking for is young, blond, and—"

"Light a shuck," I said.

He started, walked a half-dozen steps, then turned. "I'm a Pinkerton man. I'll be in Parrott City, and the offer stands. Fifty dollars is two months' wages for a cowhand."

He walked away and I listened to his footsteps on the trail until they died away. Shortly after, I heard a horse walking away. Listening until the sound died out, I walked across the road to the granary and turned in.

A Pinkerton man, looking for a young, blond woman? He evidently did not know there were two women here and he had believed the woman he sought owned the ranch. Now why was he looking for Matty, if that was who it was? Detectives often searched for people for other reasons than crimes.

At daylight I walked up the road to where he'd tied his horse. He had come from the east, probably Animas City, and had walked his horse in the grass along the shoulder of the trail until well past the house. He had gotten past the house without my hearing him and had tied his mount, then walked back down, probably to look in the windows. By the time he was close the lights had gone out. He had ridden east when he left, and the closest place would be Parrott City.

Irritated, I walked back to the house and breakfast. I was upset with myself at being so careless as to let a rider pass without my knowing it. A thing like that could get a man killed. It showed what good food and womenfolks could do to a man. Take his mind off the things he'd best pay a mind to.

My breakfast was on the table when I came in but neither of the women was around. I ate alone, hurried it up, and then went outside. I'd planned on makin' a partial count of the cattle on the place, but after that visit last night I figured I'd better stay around the home place. There was plenty to do.

McCarron, the hand Burrows had killed, had rounded up some saddle stock and brought it in to a corral near the barn. They hadn't been ridden much, aside from the two head they kept in the barn for the women to ride. I'd need something to spare the roan, so I saddled up a couple of the broncs in the corral, and although pretty feisty at first they gentled down pretty good. One of them was a black gelding with a white face, and I brought him in for the morning ride.

The roan didn't like it much. He tossed his head and trotted along the corral fence keeping pace with us and wanting to go. As the ranch house was at the lowest place on the ranch, I could ride a good part of the nearby range without getting out of sight of the house. Taking my time, I cleaned out a water hole, stacked some fallen-down branches for firewood, and generally kept a watch on the trail.

A couple of buckboards passed, and a spring wagon coming from the west, evidently headed for Animas City. There was no sign of my visitor of the previous night.

Had he given up? I doubted that, knowing the breed. He would inquire around and come upon some cowboy or miner who knew Matty was living at the ranch. Then he would come back again. The men Pinkerton hired were tough men, and they were stayers. This one had been a cool customer and wasn't going to be stampeded by anyone or anything.

We needed a dog and we needed another man. There'd be times when I wouldn't be around. The trouble was I didn't know anybody in this neck of the woods unless somebody drifted in rustling work. If I was ever going to reclaim my outfit I'd have to get back along the trail and pick it up and pay for the keep of my horses.

Mrs. Hollyrood was in the kitchen when I entered. It was just shy of noon. Matty was nowhere to be seen.

"Are you hungry? Matty made sandwiches, and there's coffee."

"It'll do me." I sat down and she brought a couple of thick

sandwiches to the table and poured coffee. "You hear all that talk last night?"

She stopped, coffeepot in hand. "Talk?"

"After you went to bed, when the lights were out. There was a man out there, said he was a Pink. A Pinkerton."

"You mean a detective? *Here?*"

The laughter that always seemed to lurk behind her eyes had vanished. The eyes were cool, speculative. "Just what did he want?"

"He was asking about a young woman, a young, blond woman. He seemed to have the idea she was the owner here."

The room was quiet. Hungry, I bit into my sandwich. It was good, mighty good. Mrs. Hollyrood looked out the window, up the road to the east, and what she was thinking I had no idea.

"Did he say why he looked for her?"

"No. The fact is that I sent him on his way. It was late and I was afraid our talking would wake you up, if you were asleep."

"He's gone then?"

"No, ma'am. He'll be back. You understand, I didn't see him in daylight, but that's a tough man. He'll be back until he finds what he's lookin' for, whatever that is."

"A young, blond woman? Did he describe Matty? Did he have a name?"

"He didn't have time."

Her face was partly turned from me and I could read nothing in it. If she was scared or worried she did not show it at all.

"Ma'am? Over there where they tried to hang me I left an outfit. I mean I had two horses and some gear, tools, bedding, an' such. One of these days I'm going to ride over there and pick it up."

"You'll be gone then?"

"For a few days. I reckon a week. When I rode over this away I was travelin' mighty fast. I figured there'd be a posse right behind me and I stretched out. That roan, I love that horse, ma'am, that roan did what would have killed most horses. I wasn't makin' any great show of it but I was putting a lot of country behind me. What I covered in two days an' most of a night would take me easy four days riding sensible."

"We will miss you, and I wish—I wish you'd not leave for a day or two. I mean with this detective . . . I don't know what to think about him. I wish you'd stay on."

"That I can do."

Pushing back my chair, I made as if to get up, but she asked me to stay, so I relaxed, sort of. But my eyes were on the road outside. To tell the truth I was worried about that detective. He was a hard, sharp man and he was, like I remembered the Pinkertons, a stayer. He was not one to give up, and I was worried for Matty. If it was her he was looking for, which I doubted.

When a man starts hunting for somebody with few clues he just naturally follows any lead he can find, and if somebody told him about a young blond woman newly arrived at a ranch, he would surely investigate. Chances are when he had looked at her he would realize he was wrong and ride on about his business.

"That young man who was out here? The one who said he was Mr. Phillips' nephew? What was his full name? The one they called Lew?"

"Paine. Lew Paine. I know nothing else about him. In fact, I don't recall Mr. Phillips ever mentioning him."

"He may not have liked him. There's no reason why a man has to like all his relatives or why they should like him."

Mrs. Hollyrood must have been a really beautiful woman when she was young. Not that I know much about women or have been associated with them very much. She was a handsome woman even now. She looked soft, warm, and pleasant. Her gray hair always as neat as could be. It was no wonder that Mr. Phillips was taken with her, and I suspected had he lived he would have been popping the question.

"Mr. Phillips?" I asked. "What sort of man was he?"

She glanced at me, then said, "Why, most pleasant! More like a businessman than a rancher. He dressed very well, always neat. And he was very much the gentleman although perhaps a little old-fashioned. I liked him."

"He surely liked you, to leave all this ranch to you."

"I don't believe there was anyone else. I did not know about the nephew, and Mr. Phillips never mentioned him. That was how I came to the conclusion they did not get along."

She frowned a little. "He seemed to have no financial worries, and since coming here I've wondered if he did not have some source of income other than this ranch. Although he may have made a sale of some of his cattle—"

"I don't think so. I mean there's cattle out there he'd prob'ly have sold if he was making a drive." I reached for my hat. "Where'd you meet him, ma'am?"

"In Kansas City. He came every night to the theater."

"And the last time you saw him?"

"In Denver, at the Brown Palace. He always stayed there, and as you know it was the place where big cattlemen stayed, and mining men as well."

I wanted to ask where she actually met Matty, but shied away from it. Certainly it was none of my affair, but since this Pink was on somebody's trail it had me worried. Anyway, it was probably some other blond young woman. There were a lot of them around.

Taking my hat I got up. "If that Pinkerton man comes around again, do you want to see him?"

She hesitated, and again I wondered where Matty was and if she could hear us. "If necessary. To tell you the truth, I'd rather not." She glanced at me. "You did not mention Matty?"

"No, ma'am, I didn't. I didn't at all."

Outside, I turned my hat in my hands and wiped off the sweatband, although it didn't need it. Somehow the conversation worried me.

Did she not want to meet the Pinkerton? Or was it Matty?

Surely they needed somebody to take care of them, and I'll bet right now they were wishing Mr. Phillips was still alive. He would have known what to do.

Me, I was all right when it came to shootin'.

SEVEN

There was plenty to do and I was a man accustomed to hard work. This here was piddling stuff, yet I enjoyed the doing of it. Never did I work for any rawhide outfit and I wasn't about to begin. There's no stopping of work on a ranch. There's always something needs doing.

Each day I used a different horse in the morning and at noon, trying to keep them in shape for riding. Meanwhile I kept an eye on the road.

A lot of folks went by. When I say a lot, I mean five or six a day and occasional freight wagons hauling to Parrott City or over to the Mormon settlements westward.

Time to time I passed the time of day with folks on the trail. The railroad was building toward Animas City but there was some difficulty about where and how they would build. Folks in Animas City had some big ideas about how much the railroad would do for their town and how much they'd get for their land.

Three days went by and I was waiting for the other shoe to drop. That Pinkerton man hadn't been back. More than likely he'd found he was mistaken and had gone on about his business. Just about the time I decided that, I was forking hay to the stock and I saw him. He was riding a bay horse and seemed to be driving right along the road.

I stuck the fork down in the hay and walked to the road. He pulled up when he saw me.

"Howdy." He had a cold eye. "You the gent I talked to the other evenin'?"

"I'd say so."

"You always wear a gun at work?"

42

"It's a tool. A man never knows when he'll need his tools. You find who you're lookin' for?"

"Not yet."

"Lots of good country west of here. Far's that goes, there's country east, north, an' south, too. No use a man confinin' himself."

"What do they call you?"

Well, I looked at him. "Nobody has to call me more than once," I said.

"I'm not hunting trouble. I am looking for a woman. She's wanted."

"Most women are," I said, "by somebody, somewhere. If you keep travelin' you might find one that wants you."

He studied me carefully. "You look to me like a man who could take care of himself with men. How are you with women?"

"Nobody never complained, an' I've known a few here an' there."

"Nice spread." He turned in the saddle, glancing around.

"Needs work," I said. "I been fixin' up around. I hate to see a place run down."

"So do I. Hard for a woman to keep a place like this."

"Uh-huh. I doubt if Phillips had been doin' much on the place himself. Or else he didn't want to spend money on hands. I'll shape it up some before I ride on."

He studied me. "To where?"

"The San Juans, maybe."

"This woman you're working for? Elderly, you say?"

"I don't recall sayin'. She's got gray hair. Doesn't get around very much."

Somebody was behind a curtain in the window. I'd seen it move a mite. We were too far away for anybody to hear what we were sayin', but whoever was watching could see us talkin'.

"I don't see much of them," I said. "I'm gettin' the place into shape an' then I'm ridin' on. After all"—I grinned at him—"I'm just passin' through."

When I smiled he glanced at me. "Something funny about that?"

"It's what folks call me. 'Passin' Through.'"

"If I were you," he said, "I'd just live up to the name."

With that he clucked to his horse, touched his heels to the

gelding's ribs, and trotted off along the trail. Standing there, I watched him go, wondering about him.

Suddenly, I went to the corral and dabbed a loop on a buckskin, led him to the rail, and saddled up. When I rode him over to the house, Matty met me at the door.

"Thought I'd meander along to Parrott City," I said, "look at the city lights. Anything I can get you in town?"

"What did that man want?"

"Snoopin', mostly." Hesitating, I then added, "He's huntin' a woman, a young, blond woman."

She studied me. "You believe he is looking for me? Is that it?"

"No, ma'am, I don't. I think he's lookin' for some other woman and when he heard there were women here he decided to sort of check it out."

"Did he say why he was looking for her?"

"I didn't expect him to. His kind are lookin' for information, not givin' it out."

She gave me a list, not a long one. "What I would like most are some newspapers or magazines."

"They're hard to come by, ma'am. That's what ever'body wants and they are almighty scarce. I'll see what I can do."

That blue roan led to too much talk so I had chosen the buckskin for this ride to town. The trail followed Cherry Creek for a way, then I turned off, leaving the trail and heading toward the La Platas through the scrub oak. I never did cotton to regular-traveled trails and I knew the town was tucked away close to the mountain, somewhere almost due north.

From time to time I drew up to study the country. This was get-acquainted time and I knew too little of the country. Setting my horse amongst the brush, I could look back across at a high peak and the fine sweep of land that comprised the ranch. Toward the top of the peak, crested with ponderosa, there was a thick stand of aspen and a lovely draw that ran up from the creek to a saddle just west of the highest point. It was surely beautiful country, and I don't mind thinking how much I envied Mrs. Hollyrood, owning that place.

The buckskin was a good horse and he took to rough country like he was born to it, which he probably was. I'd known of Parrott City before ever I left Pioche. John Moss had laid out the town about 1875 when he was prospecting for Tiburcio Parrott, a banker in San Francisco. Wherever miners or prospectors gather there is talk of new strikes, new mining towns, or trails leading to good prospects. The La Platas were much talked about, as, of course, were the San Juans, only a bit further along. Silverton was a booming camp, but that was sixty or seventy miles away over rough mountain trails.

When I rode up the street in Parrott City it took me no time at all to see what was available. There were a couple of saloons, a blacksmith shop where most of the work was sharpening drill steel, and there was a general supply store and a couple of tents which rented out beds. I guess there were ten to twelve buildings in town and some makeshift squatters' shacks. But nobody had promised me another Denver.

At the store I bought a packet of pins and some needles for Matty and a couple of shirts for myself as well as a new pair of pants. Nobody seemed to pay me much mind until I paid my bill, and then the storekeeper asked me if I was a miner.

"I've mined," I said, "mostly for myself." Before he could ask any more questions I took my goods and walked outside, looking up at the mountain. This was mighty pretty country and La Plata Canyon invited a man to try his luck.

Standing on the street, I sort of looked the town over, and there wasn't enough of it to take a man more than a few minutes. That Pinkerton man was somewhere about and I wanted to learn more about him.

There was a two-by-four sort of place across the street where they served meals and I crossed over and went in. An un-shaved man in shirt sleeves was washing dishes back of the counter, which was just a couple of planks nailed together with a bench in front of it. There were also two tables. "Am I late for grub?"

"Hell, no! I've always got something on. You partial to venison stew?" He winked at me. "Least that's what I call it. Some of these folks are touchy when their cows turn up missin'."

"Well," I said, "I never heard of anybody readin' a brand from stew meat."

He chuckled. "Now you're right about that. You look like a miner."

"I've mined," I said, and keeping a straight face, I added, "Right now I'm a cattleman."

His face went blank, then he said, "That really *is* venison. Some of it."

"I'm not huntin' rustlers," I said, "and I don't own any stock hereabouts. I only hang rustlers when I catch them at it, and this is mighty fine stew. You must have cooked in a cow camp sometime or other."

"I done it," he said with satisfaction. "I went over the trail twict. Went with the big herds, first to Dodge, then to Ogallala." He looked at me again. "You been over the trail?"

"Twice," I said, "the first time when I was a youngster. I was wranglin' horses that time. Next time I was trail boss."

"Trail boss? You must've made a name for yourself."

"They knew me," I said. "It was a time of trouble."

He leaned over the counter. "Friend," he said, "you could do worse than to locate right here. Buy yourself a couple of town lots. This place will boom. Take it from me. There's rich mines all about here, an' La Plata County was set up in 1874. This here's the county seat. Get in on the ground floor if you've got any capital.

"I own four city lots," he added, "an' I've staked some ground up the canyon."

"I was just passin' through," I commented. "Stopped down on Cherry Creek to help a woman get her place in shape."

"Oh?" He looked at me again. "You're *him*? Heard about you. You the one who killed Houston Burrows?"

News had a way of travelin', and among some western people gunfighters were talked of like they were prizefighters or theater people. Nobody but some tinhorn wanted to be known as a gunfighter.

"Houston Burrows threw a wide loop," I said, "and he made the wrong catch."

The stew was good. I ate another plate of it and drank some coffee. The man behind the counter was a talker, and he felt because I'd ridden the cow trails that I was an old friend. He told me a good bit about everybody in town, all the prospects and the plans. Most of it I'd heard before about other places, because everybody who starts a town believes it will be a metropolis, eventually.

"I don't see many strangers around," I objected, "not city men, anyway."

"Ever' once in a while," he said. "You ain't here like I am. They all come in this place to eat. There's one in town right now. He doesn't have much to say but he stands around, listenin' to folks. He's some easterner, lookin' for good buys. I can tell. Fact is, he's lookin' for ranch property." The cook glanced at me. "That woman who owns the Phillips place? The one you work for? D'you think she'd sell? Hers was one of the places he was inquirin' about."

I'll bet, I said to myself, *I'll bet he asked a lot of questions.*

"She might sell," I said, "but I doubt it. She was lookin' for a place to light when she met Phillips. Been an actress," I said, knowing he'd heard it all before, "an' tired of travel. She loves this country."

Turning sidewise on the bench, I sipped my coffee, watching the street. Where was he now?

"How much?" I asked.

He spread his hands. "It's a tin roof," he said, "because you come over the trail."

" 'Tin roof'?" I asked.

He grinned. "On the house," he said. "Feller sprung that on me one time and I liked it. Next time you can pay, but this is for old times' sake."

"You can't make any money that way," I protested.

He chuckled. "Don't you worry! These lots will make me rich! You'll see! This here town will boom! John Moss started the town and he knows what he's about. It's named for this big Frisco banker, and you know darned well no Frisco banker is goin' to let his town die! But it ain't that. The mines are *rich*! Rich, I tell you.

"Then there's cattle. Lots of men running cattle. Feller named Caviness come in with a big herd. Thompson, too. He's in that cove just west of where you're located.

"Some towns are minin', some are cow towns, but this has it all, minin', cattle, sheep, an' now the railroad."

"That's comin' to Animas City, I hear."

"Oh, sure! That's what they say, and it will, but do you think they'd pass up a boomin' town like this? They'll be in here within the year. You just wait an' see!"

A buckboard was tied up across the street, and a man and woman were getting down from it. Walking across, I untied my horse, glancing at the woman as I did so. She was young, quite pretty, and a city woman. The man with her looked like a businessman or an official of some kind. She gave me a quick look, then looked again. I tipped my hat and she looked quickly away, flushing a little. Stepping into the saddle, I rode out of town.

When I saw an opening in the scrub oak I rode through,

taking a route a half-mile or so to the east of that I had taken
when riding to Parrott City, so as not to follow the same route
on my return. Several times I drew up, listening, and when-
ever possible checked my back trail by sitting my horse and
watching the few open areas I'd crossed. Soon I was working
my way through and around stands of ponderosa or aspen until
I found myself in a clearing on the mountainside with a tre-
mendous view of the ranch. Drawing rein, while sitting horse
under a couple of tall pines, I studied the layout.

Backed by the long ridge, at least a thousand feet higher
than the ranch buildings, it was a green and lovely place with
several wooded knolls like thick fingers reaching out from the
ridge toward Cherry Creek and the trail.

Between the knolls were meadows with fine stands of grass.
As I sat my saddle studying the place I saw three riders come
from under the trees on the highest part of the ridge opposite.
From where they were they had a great view of the ranch and
of my area as well, but I was well back in the shadow of the
pines and, I hoped, invisible to them, as long as I remained
still.

One of the riders was astride a black horse with a splash of
white over its rump. The man who had come to the ranch with
Lew Paine had ridden such a horse, the man who had placed the
noose around my neck.

They were a good half-mile away, and as I watched they
began to ride along the ridge, dipping down into the saddle,
riding west and closer to the ranch. There were trails from the
ridge to the meadows, as I'd seen one of them. They dipped
into the trees and I lost them.

Keeping under cover, I headed for the ranch. What they had
in mind I did not know, but when they arrived, I'd be waiting.

Waiting, and with a Winchester . . .

EIGHT

The buckskin would be hard to see against the mottled greens and browns of the mountainside, and my clothes were nondescript. Keeping under the shelter of the ponderosa, I wove a course west above the trail, then dipped down into a draw that ended behind the house.

Unfortunately, I startled a deer feeding on the slope behind the house, but he ran off just a few yards and stopped, looking around. When it seemed obvious I wasn't on the hunt, he just went to feeding again.

Lazy smoke rose from the chimney and I stepped down from the saddle and went to the side door, leaving my horse tied to a willow tree back of the house. Winchester in hand, I knocked on the door.

Matty opened it. "Trouble coming," I said. "I wanted you should know."

"That detective again?"

"Lew Paine and a couple of riders. They're up on the ridge but they're keeping from sight and I don't know what they have in mind. You folks keep quiet and out of sight."

Taking a chair, I sat back inside the window but where I could keep a watch. There was a low ridge back of the creek that worried me some but it did not offer much cover. It did provide an easy place to watch the house and within easy rifle range. They could get to it without me seeing them. If they came down the meadow and around the end of the ridge I'd have them covered. There was a place back the way I'd come that would allow me to cover that ridge. I got up. "Just wanted you to know. No matter what happens, you folks stay inside. I'll be around doin' what's needful."

49

Taking my rifle, I went back to the buckskin, mounted, and went back along the draw I'd followed from up on the mountain. When some scrub oak and a cedar tree offered cover, I rode up out of the draw and into the trees. Tying my horse to some brush, I went down through the trees until I found the spot I wanted.

It was a warm, clear day. A few puffballs of cloud floated about, as they nearly always did in this country, and it was pleasant setting there, smelling the pines. There was a litter of pinecones among the needles on the ground, and away from the trees the tall grass moved when stirred by the wind.

They came out of the trees at the head of the meadow, then crossed to the near side where I could no longer see them. What they had in mind I'd no idea, unless they meant to try and scare the womenfolks. They knew I wouldn't scare, but they might not know I'd returned from Parrott City.

When they reached the end of the concealment offered by one of those long knolls they stepped down from their horses and led them, keeping to low ground and heading for that ridge. There was some low brush on the ridge, and a few scattered trees. I'd had a look at the ridge when I first rode around on the ranch and knew it was rocky ground with only thin grass.

A magpie lit on a low branch near me and cocked his head at me, trying to decide whether my being there was reason enough to make a fuss. Finally, after pecking at a few items in the grass he flew off about his business, and I eased the rifle from the ground, keeping it out of the sunlight as I wanted no flash from sunlight on the barrel to warn them.

They'd found the place they wanted, and Lew Paine rested his rifle in the crotch of a small oak and tucked the butt against his shoulder. When he done that, I squeezed off a shot. Now, I was of no mind to kill him unless he made it necessary, but I knew what I could do with a rifle, and my bullet slapped that tree trunk right close to his face. Of course, he might have moved into my line of fire, but he didn't. That bullet spat bark fragments in his face and he dropped his rifle like it was red-hot and hit the dirt.

Just for luck I moved over a few paces and put a bullet into the dirt under one man's feet. It was that same gent who looped the rope over my head at the hangin'.

Well, they left out of there. They'd come to scare some

women, not to be shot at themselves. They hit their saddles like they'd been scalded and they raised some dust gettin' off down the trail, afraid they'd be shot at again.

Taking two cartridges from my belt, I fed them into the rifle, where I'd be apt to need them. Setting there, just resting, I thought back to that girl I'd seen over at Parrott City, and why she had looked at me as she had. She wasn't anybody I remembered knowing, although she was looking at me like she knew me. Or had she just heard talk around and was curious?

Matty was at the door when I came up on the porch. "I heard shooting?"

"They were fixin' to shoot at the house so I dusted 'em a mite to sort of change their minds."

Shadows were falling when I stripped the riggin' from the buckskin and turned it into the corral. Washing up, I studied about things and found there was something bothered me, but what it was I couldn't pin down.

Supper was laid and Matty told me to sit down and she'd have it on. From my pocket I took the pins and needles I'd picked up for her and she thanked me. "It isn't much of a town," I explained, "supplies are limited. More fixin's for miners than anything else, but there's some grub. Groceries, I mean. Not much to interest a woman."

"We've not been over there," Matty said. "We did drive into Animas City once, but it is such a long drive and we didn't like to be away from the place.

"It's so different here than Mrs. Hollyrood expected. When Mr. Phillips spoke of his ranch, she always thought of it like a southern plantation with a big house, white pillars and all that, with a fine carriage and driving horses. She just didn't know what a ranch could be like, and neither did I."

"Pretty rough by your standards," I suggested. "Folks out here have to make do. This house is better than most. The logs were squared off by somebody who knew how to use an adze and a broadax. The granary and barn were built by the same hand. It shows in the workmanship.

"It's a fine place," I said, "but to make any money out of it the owner has to know cattle or somebody who does. I can see where she must have been surprised."

She put a plate before me and I set to. Bein' hungry, I wasted no time. Then I said, "Didn't Phillips tell you what the ranch was like?"

"I scarcely knew him. Yes, he told us about it, but Mrs. Hollyrood had never seen a western ranch and thought of it in different terms. When we were coming out on the train she said we'd have a good life here, and hoped the servants would be the sort she wanted to keep. I believe she was expecting much more."

"It's a rough life," I agreed, "but there's some fine folks in the country around. I mean, good substantial people, all of them working to make something of their land or the mines or whatever."

"I believe she's thinking about selling."

Well, I swallowed what I had in my mouth and waited a minute whilst she filled my cup. "I haven't asked around," I said, "but I'd not imagine she could get much of a price. This here is good land but mostly for cattle or sheep. There's a man over west of here has done well planting barley and oats, but you have to know what you're doing. To tell you the truth, ma'am, I doubt if you could get more for the place than it would cost you to go back east."

"I don't believe that." It was Mrs. Hollyrood, wearing another one of those dressin' gowns she wore all the time. "This is good land, and I am sure someone would wish to buy it."

"Water controls the land, ma'am. You've a good spring here and Cherry Creek runnin' through. My guess is you'd be lucky to get ten dollars an acre for it.

"Eighteen eighty-one has started off slow around here, ma'am, and there's so much free land that cattle or sheep men just don't have to buy. Folks who have money to spend will be buying lots in town now the railroad is comin' in. There's talk the railroad will build its own town an' leave Animas City high and dry. But don't take that for gospel. I just listen when folks talk."

"Do they talk about this place? About me?"

"No, ma'am, not that I heard. Folks are pretty busy with their own affairs. Naturally, your bein' new folks I expect there's some curiosity. And that Pinkerton man, he's been askin' questions."

Her skin seemed to tighten and for a moment there she looked almost angry. First time I'd seen anything but pleasantness on her face.

"You brought back a few things," she said, "and I thank you. I am afraid there is too little here." She looked over at me suddenly. "You spoke of cattle. Have you any idea how many could be sold?"

"It's mostly young stuff, ma'am, just what you need to start a ranchin' operation. With what I've seen, an' I haven't been over but a piece of country, you've got the makin's of a fine little ranch here. Why, in four or five years—"

"Four or five *years*?" she exclaimed. "But that's impossible! I can't spend that much time here. Why—!" She shook her head. "Mr. Passin', you'll simply have to help us. We know nothing about ranching, and when we came here . . . well, we didn't expect *this*. All we can do is sell the cattle and the ranch, whatever there is, and go back east.

"I'm afraid I'm not cut out for this, Mr. Passin'. I've been accustomed to people, to lights, music, crowds. I thought when we came here it would be a place to rest, to recuperate. All I can see ahead of us here is a lot of hard work."

"That's true, ma'am. It's a good place but it will need work. There's nothing about this country that's easy, there's aplenty here but it has to be worked for. Nobody hands it to you on a platter."

"But isn't there gold out here? Mightn't there be gold on this property?"

"I doubt it, ma'am. There's gold in the La Platas, and there's silver, as the old Spanishmen who named the mountains knew, but it takes a sight of work to get at it. This land you've got . . . well, up there on the hill I saw an outcropping of coal. May not amount to much, and folks over in Pioche told me there was a lot of coal in this country, but nobody is buyin' coal from out here. Maybe after the railroad is in . . . but there's plenty of it easier to mine and closer to the railroad.

"You'll have to make it with cattle, ma'am. Or sheep."

"Find a buyer for me. I will sell the cattle and the ranch. We will sell out and go east."

"Like I say, ma'am, that will take some doin'. There's still land around for the takin', I expect, although I've made no inquiries and cash money is almighty scarce."

She seemed some put out. She got up and walked to the window, but all you could see from there was the black ridge against the sky and some stars that looked like lights not far off, bright as they were in the night sky.

"There's beauty here, ma'am. It's a great country. Over yonder on the east side of this place there's a fine stand of aspen. They'll turn gold in the autumn, ma'am, and the oak will turn red, some of it. Ma'am, just wait until you see it. You'll never want to leave."

Well, she just looked at me. "I shall want to leave, young man, and I shall do so. Find me a buyer." She turned her eyes to me with a quizzical look. "Unless you'd like to buy it yourself. You said you'd saved a little."

Well, I blushed. At least I turned kind of red. I could feel it. "Ma'am, my little stake wouldn't count to a hill of beans. I'm a workin' man, ma'am, and I never had much. This bit I got put by is nothing. I couldn't begin to buy this ranch or the cattle."

"I want to leave. I might sell for less than you expect."

"You've called me Mr. Passin', Passin' Through, that's me. I was driftin' when I came here and when I leave I'll just keep on down the trail. I came from nowhere and I'm goin' right back."

"You have no relatives? No one who would miss you?"

"Not a soul, ma'am. I'm a lone-ridin' man an' there's nobody waitin' for me, anywhere."

Matty was staring at me, almost angry, it seemed like. Anyway, she was irritated. About what I didn't know. Maybe she thought I was feelin' sorry for myself, but no such thing. It was just my way of talkin'. This was the kind of life I liked.

Well, I finished eating and went to the granary. I saw Mrs. Hollyrood get up and go to her room, and Matty was revving up in the kitchen.

For some reason I was unhappy with myself, and I leaned on the corral bars and the roan came over and pushed its nose against me. Why I should be out of sorts I didn't know, unless it was the thought of them selling this place.

Good land was getting scarce with all the folks moving in, and this was one of the last places in the country to be settled. Somehow I'd thought they'd come home. I mean, that this was where they'd stay. If I'd figured they were just going to sell out and move on, I'd not have been so all-fired busy fixing things up.

Matty came to the door and threw out some water, then she walked over to me. She stood there a minute, enjoying the night.

"It *is* beautiful," she said.

"Yes, ma'am. Rarely so, rarely. Somehow I wasn't expectin' you folks to move on. I thought you'd found a home."

"Mr. Passin'," she spoke quietly, "no matter what you think of yourself you're a nice man, a kindly man. If I were you I'd saddle up that roan and ride out of here, and I would do it now. I would ride out and never look back."

She walked back to the house, into the door, and a moment later the light was blown out.

Well, now. That was a surprise. Ride out, when they still had trouble facin' them? Ride out when Lew Paine was still around? I couldn't do that.

I went inside and undressed for bed. When I had a boot off I sat on the edge of the bed thinkin' of what she'd said, and wonderin' why. It sounded almost like a warnin', and no doubt she didn't see much sense in me bein' involved with their troubles with Lew Paine, and all.

Daybreak showed up right on time and found me out there giving the horses a bait of corn as well as hay. This was a day I planned on checking cattle, but first I needed to see Phillips' tally book, if he left one.

Most cowmen keep a tally of the cattle on the range and the brands they own or see on their place. Some cattlemen had several brands registered in their name, as often enough they'd buy out another brand. If I had his tally book I could have an idea of what to look for and how many.

Breakfast was soon over and Matty came in as I was finishing. She'd left everything ready for me.

"Ma'am? A cattleman usually has a tally book that keeps account of the cattle he owns and the brands. Usually it's a little notebook, bound in leather or cloth or somethin' of the kind."

"There's some old papers in that drawer over there, on the far side of the living room. I don't know what all it is, just old letters and such. I believe I did see a little brown book in there."

Takin' my cup with me, I went in to where the drawer was and opened it. Sure enough, there was a sheaf of papers there, mostly old. There was the tally book that I wanted, but I gathered up all of it.

When I got back to my bunk in the granary I sat down and opened up the tally book. What I wanted was there all right, but there was something else.

There was a will, a last will and testament.

NINE

Matty had been busy at the cookin' stove when I gathered up the papers and I'd put most of them in the pocket of my coat. Holding up the tally book, I'd said, "This was what I wanted. Now I can get some idea of what to look for."

Every cattleman had his own way of keeping accounts—some were mighty casual about it, others very thorough. Often they wrote in a shorthand of their own, not to conceal anything but just to keep it brief. Some items were dated as to where cattle had been seen, and I found mention of two springs or seeps I hadn't known about.

"Now I'll be able to get some idea of what the place is worth," I'd told her, "although I think she'd be foolish to sell. The deeded land is worth something, but there's a lot of grazin' around, all for free."

"We know nothing about cattle and Mrs. Hollyrood only planned to vacation here. She wanted to rest and relax. This"— she glanced around—"wasn't exactly what she expected."

Matty was wearin' a blue-an'-white gingham dress an' looked mighty fetchin'. Her eyes were very large and she had a way of lookin' directly at you, but she rarely smiled. Her face was without a line that I could see.

There was something about her that was somehow familiar although I knew I'd never seen her before. Something in her voice, something in the way she walked.

Checking through the tally book, I made a rough count in my head and figured there must be six or seven hundred head of mixed stock runnin' around. From what I'd seen it didn't look like he'd shipped lately. That is, I'd seen thirty or forty

56

head, just in my few rides, that were the right age and size. If he had sold very much, this stock would have gone along with the rest.

He had some fat young stuff that was coming along, and with the railroad coming in he stood to make some cash money. Looked to me, thinking of that stock ready for shipping, that he had known about the railroad and was waiting a-purpose.

"Mrs. Hollyrood would like to realize as much cash as she can and just go back where she came from."

Well, I could understand that. For her kind of woman this wasn't much of a life. She was used to the city, theaters, and living high off the hog.

"How about you?" I asked. "She could let you run this place. I can't stay on, but I'd help you get started, and then go on about my business."

"You're a mining man?"

"Not really, ma'am. I've worked at this an' that, but I've prospected some and mostly found nothing. Sometimes a man will find a pocket, but when he's cleaned it out there's not much left. I found one here a month or so back. Did pretty well."

Taking up my hat and stuffing the tally book in my pocket, I thanked her for breakfast and went to the granary. Findin' that will in the drawer bothered me some. It had been shuffled in with a lot of old letters and could easily have been missed.

Alone in the granary I sat on my bunk and looked at that will. With the first line I shivered like somebody had stepped on my grave.

I, John Le Caudy Phillips, being of sound mind, do hereby give and bequeath all my worldly possessions to my beloved niece, Janet Le Caudy. Her father, Robert Le Caudy, having left her his half-share in the ranch and cattle, this leaves her the entire and exclusive ownership of the properties concerned.

It was signed by Phillips and witnessed by three men, Jacob Reams, William Barker, and Timothy Farrell.

For a long time I just stared at that will. Something was very wrong here. If this will was a true one, then the will that gave the ranch to Mrs. Hollyrood was not. And who was Janet Le Caudy, "my beloved niece"?

My attention returned to the will. It was dated in Animas City, just one year ago. What was the date on the will Mrs. Hollyrood possessed? Something was wrong here, very wrong.

If Phillips had left the ranch to Mrs. Hollyrood, what of "my beloved niece"? And what of the half of the ranch she owned, anyway?

Lawing had never been any part of my business. Like many another, I'd picked up a little law from hearing it argued in court, but that wasn't near enough.

How did all these papers happen to be in that drawer? Had Mrs. Hollyrood and Matty never searched the house? It stood to reason they had not. Matty knew the papers were there, she'd told me of them. Evidently looking through dusty papers in an old ranch-house desk hadn't appealed to them. Probably they felt they were of no concern.

Taking up the letters, I glanced through them. Most were from this Janet. He called her Jackie, and from the tone Phillips had been more like a father than an uncle. The letters from her showed a genuine affection, and it looked like Phillips had financed her education and such. A man like that wouldn't be about to disown a niece he loved so much. Yet, he had done just that. Was this what lawyers might call "undue influence"? I mean, had Mrs. Hollyrood had him so taken with her that he forgot his niece? But how could he forget that she owned half the ranch?

He couldn't legally give away something he didn't own, no matter how involved he might have been.

Now I was worried. Looking down at the stuff in my hands, I had an idea. Several business letters were in the bunch, so I left them out in plain sight but arranged them so I'd know if anybody touched them. Some I took from the envelopes and scattered them to make it look like more than there were. The other letters and the will I put in a rusty tin can and sat it on a beam in the dark with a few rusty nails atop of it.

With the tally book I set out to check the range, counting cattle as I rode. By the time the sun was sliding down the western sky I had counted a hundred and forty head of longhorns, all in pretty good shape, and sixty-five head of whiteface cattle. When I turned my mount into the corral, I washed up but found myself hesitating about going inside. Finally, I walked over, rapped on the door, and stepped inside.

Supper was on and Matty looked around from the stove. "You're late."

"Yes, ma'am. I was countin' cattle. You've got some fine

stock out there. This is good grazin' land and the stock I saw is nice 'n' fat."

Mrs. Hollyrood came in, her gray hair lookin' like she just had a hairdresser work on it. But then, she always looked neat an' proper. "Matty tells me you found the tally book—was that what you called it?"

"Yes, ma'am. It helps a good bit. Now I know how many head he was runnin' and where most of them graze. A few days from now I'll have an accurate count for you."

"Can you arrange a sale? I don't necessarily mean to ship them, but perhaps some of the local ranchers would be interested."

"They sure would, ma'am, but cash money is almighty scarce. I doubt if there's anybody around who could pay cash on the barrelhead for them. Nobody has that kind of money lyin' about."

"How about you, Mr. Passin'?"

"No, ma'am, I'm not fixed to go into the cattle business. I got me a little stake but not enough to handle a deal like that. Anyway, I'm driftin'. This here's mighty pretty country but there's a sight of land I haven't seen. I'm ridin' back to get my horses and gear an' then I'll hit the trail."

Pausing, I looked around at her. "Ain't much I can do for you folks once I've finished my count. There's no use fixin' up around if you're not plannin' to stay."

Well, we set there talkin' of this an' that, and finally Mrs. Hollyrood, she says, "You've been very kind, Mr. Passin'. Let us know when you plan to leave and I'll fix a nice supper for you."

"Thank you, ma'am. I'd appreciate that."

It was a beautiful starlit night and all of a sudden I was wishing I was out on the trail, makin' my own camp, goin' to sleep with the stars overhead and a breeze stirrin' the aspens.

Maybe I wasn't much of a people man. Maybe I was just fixed for the out-of-doors, for the wide open country where the coyotes run and the eagles fly.

At the door I took down my lantern, lifted the globe, and struck a match to light the wick. Then I went inside. I hung up the lantern and taken off my jacket. As I hung it up my eyes went to the table where I'd left the letters and for a moment I stood real still, just lookin'. Somebody had moved them, moved them carefully so's they thought I'd not notice. But I'd left them so I would know.

A person lookin' at such truck would leave it much as it was found, but disarranged. Whoever had looked at those letters had tried to leave them exactly as I'd left them.

Standing where I was, I looked around, checking everything. Now, I'd been makin' my bed army-style the way McCarron left it, the top blanket tight enough to bounce a coin on it. It was made up the same way but wasn't nowhere near as tight as I'd left it.

Somebody had looked under my pillow and had examined the bed, somebody who tried to leave it so's I'd not know they'd been around.

The spare pistol I left in the bed was still there and I picked it up. Now, when a man handles guns ever' day of his life he comes to know their feel, and something about this one, my own gun, felt wrong. Mostly I carried a Colt, but this was a new gun I'd picked up. I swung out the cylinder to check it, and started to close it again when something caught my eye. I looked again.

Now I always kept my guns full loaded. Some left an empty chamber under the hammer, but not me. When I wanted a gun I wanted it bad, and this one was loaded, but something caught my eye and I knew I was lookin' at an exploded shell. Now, when I fire a shot I reload. I never left a gun with empty shells in it.

Dumping these out in my hand, I swore softly, bitterly. Somebody wanted me dead. Somebody who had removed three cartridges from my gun and substituted three empty shells placed so the next three shots I tried to fire would be wasted.

Somebody who had access to the granary and my bunk wanted me dead, no matter where or by whom.

It was time I was getting off down the trail. One thing I wanted, and they had offered to pay me. I wanted the Death Horse. I wanted that blue roan. That was a mighty fine animal and left here somebody would shoot it, feelin' as they did. Maybe that horse would carry me to my death, but if so it would be a mighty nice ride.

Right then I made up my mind. I was gettin' out of here. No reason why I should stay. I'd stopped figurin' to help a couple of lone women fix up their outfit, but it seems they were gettin' shut of the place anyway.

Gatherin' up the letters, I put them in a bundle, but after I'd put the light out so's nobody could see what I was doing, I climbed up and checked my tin can where I'd hid the will. It was there, undisturbed. I put it back.

That Pinkerton man, now, he had never actually said what he was lookin' for or who sent him. If he was still in Parrott City I'd look him up. Also, I'd get what I needed for the trail. I was gettin' out, goin' on down the road.

When I saddled up, I chose the roan, and the horse seemed pleased. I roughed up the hair on his back a little, scratchin' him around the ears, too. Then I smoothed out the hair on his back and threw the saddle on him. All the time I was thinkin', tryin' to work my way out of the woods. What to do about that will worried me.

Mrs. Hollyrood had inherited the property with a will written by Phillips. She had come in and taken possession of it, satisfying the sheriff and the local judge that her claim was just. Now I'd found this other will, and it didn't seem logical that a man who spoke of his beloved niece would then disinherit her without so much as a mention.

Rightly speakin' it was none of my affair, and I had troubles enough of my own. Nobody needed to tell me that I hadn't seen the last of the Burrows outfit. They'd get all liquored up someday an' come huntin' my scalp.

Moreover, I wanted my two horses and my gear, and if I went after them I'd be walkin' right into trouble. Yet I was a stubborn sort of feller and wanted what was mine.

Matty came to the door when I led the roan out to mount up. "Will you be gone today?"

"No, ma'am. Just ridin' up the road a piece." I hesitated. "By the way, you an' Mrs. Hollyrood both wanted to pay me for the work I've done, and neither of you or anybody else wanted this roan. If you still want to pay, why not just give me a bill of sale on the roan and we'll call it quits."

"I'll ask her." She came down to where I stood and spoke softly. "If you're going, go quickly. I don't mean now, I mean leave the ranch. Get away from here."

I made as if I was tightening the cinch. "Any pa'tic'lar reason?"

"Just go. Don't ask questions." She turned away, then looked back. "You're a nice man. I don't believe you should mix into other people's troubles. Go . . . please go!"

Well, I stepped into the leather and waved to her. "Tell Mrs. Hollyrood I'm ridin' into Parrott City to see if I can find that buyer you're askin' about."

A half-mile up the trail I saw a camp alongside Cherry Creek. It was a man with two horses. He was wearin' a suit and had his pants tucked down into his boot tops, and a narrow-brimmed hat. It was the Pink. I walked my horse down to where he had his fire.

"You're on private property," I said, "but as long as you don't let that fire get away we won't complain."

"You planning to stay around? If I were you I'd give it some thought. Those Burrows boys are some upset. Sooner or later they'll be coming after you."

"Well, I ain't huntin' trouble, but if they come after me they'll find it. I don't run very well, an' neither does my horse."

"I see you're riding the Death Horse."

"Death to somebody else, not me." I stepped down from the saddle and sat down across the fire from him. "Did you find that blonde you were huntin'?"

"Would I be here if I had?"

"What d'you want her for?"

"Murder."

That shut me up. I just didn't have anything to say. Only he wasn't through.

"It may not have been the first time, and unless we find her it won't be the last."

"How old a woman?"

"Thirty, maybe thirty-five. We aren't sure, as she's covered her tracks well, but my guess is closer to thirty-five."

Right away I felt better. "The women on the ranch," I said, "wouldn't fit. The youngest one is about twenty, and the older woman, Mrs. Hollyrood, is better than fifty. I'd say about sixty. She used to be an actress."

"Mrs. Hollyrood? Never heard of her. What was her first name?"

"I never heard that. It ain't likely I would. I'm just workin' for them a mite, and I guess I've only seen her three or four times. Ate some meals with her, that's about it."

The Pink stirred the fire. "My name's Bell, Reed Bell. I've been with the agency since during the War."

"I'm called Passin' Through because that's what I'm doin'. Least, that's what Mrs. Hollyrood calls me, and I've decided I like it."

Bell studied me. "I don't remember you from any of the bulletins we get on wanted men."

"Likely not. I reckon I'm one of the most unwanted men you're apt to find.

"You say the woman you're huntin' is wanted for murder?"

"Uh-huh. She told this gent she was going to fix him a really nice supper, and she did it, too. Only the next morning he was dead."

TEN

The place he'd chosen to camp was a little hollow alongside the creek. There was a sort of a draw that ran back up the mountain to a saddle below the highest peak. It was a right pretty place.

"Nice place they've got here," Bell commented. "I'll be sorry to leave."

"You ridin' on?"

"Got to find that woman." He looked over at me. "You shape up like a man who rides for the brand. Well, in my line of work I do the same thing. I've a job to do. I've got to find that woman before she murders somebody else."

"You mean this is a pattern?"

"Not that we can prove, except in one case, but there appears to be more cases. Up to now she's been reasonably successful. She made a slip back down the line and we got the first solid evidence." He glanced over at me again. "She murdered the man she'd been working with. He was a handwriting specialist, a forger, and a good one. I guess he was greedy and wanted too much, or maybe there was a younger woman. At least, so we heard."

He finished his coffee and dumped out the pot on the fire, watched it sizzle for a moment, then kicked dirt over it. He'd built a circle of rocks around where he'd had his fire, which confined it some. There was no way it could cause trouble.

"I'm going to miss this place," I said. "It grows on a man."

Bell was saddling up. He paused, looking around at me. "You got any money?"

"A little."

"Was I you," he replied, "I'd be careful where I ate my meals."

Well, I turned the roan and rode away. Bein' a detective just naturally makes a man skeptical. Most of the time he'd be dealin' with the worst kind of folks, so he'd naturally have his doubts about anybody. If you deal with crooks all the time, pretty soon you begin to believe everybody is a crook. There were plenty of them around, but a lot of honest folks, too.

There was a kind of trail, made by deer, most likely, and it led up the mountain back of that hollow where Bell had camped. I walked the roan up the trail, weaving in and out through the scrub oak. Some of the trees had grown to fair size, but most of them were small with much undergrowth, a good place for wildlife.

Deer tracks were there aplenty, and once I glimpsed a lion track where he'd been stalking a deer. The trail widened into what was almost a lane through the aspen. It was still, no sound but the aspens moving with the slightest breeze. I drew up, listening.

A fawn came out of the aspens and walked with dainty hoofs across the land, turning its head to look at me an' the roan, but we stood quiet and it walked on, without alarm.

We walked on, heading east and away from the ranch. The trees thinned ahead of us and I could look along the trail to Animas City and beyond. The trail was empty. Frowning a little, I wondered about that. There was no way Reed Bell could have ridden out of sight along that trail, not even if he was running his horses. So where had he gone?

Suddenly uneasy, I turned my horse and scrambled up a bank and into a dense stand of aspen, weaving our way through the trees and around deadfalls into deeper cover. There I pulled up and waited, listening.

A moment, and I heard a faint stirring. A rider was coming, more than one rider. I saw a faint shadow of movement through the trees. I put a hand on the roan's neck. "Ssh!" I whispered.

They came along quietly, following my tracks. In a moment they would see where my horse had gone up the bank and into the trees.

Glancing around, I saw a narrow way where we might go. When I looked back they had pulled up and were listening. One of them offered a clear shot. I shucked my pistol.

"Looking for something?" I spoke in a low tone but loud enough for them to hear in that silence.

The nearest man jumped like he'd stepped on a cactus and whipped around, gun in hand. He saw me just as I fired. He was no more than fifty feet away, but he must have jerked back as he saw me because my bullet cut the top of his gun-filled hand, creased his chest, and went into his upper arm.

The roan started into the trees, weaving its way out of the aspens and in a dead run along the mountainside, jumping brush, ducking under tree limbs, and heading for away from there.

Behind me somebody yelled, "Get him, dammit!"

"Get him yourself!" The voice was angry. "He *got* me!"

Wheeling around a thick stand of scrub oak, I grabbed my rifle and hit the dirt running. The roan pulled up to a stand as I went into the trees. Cattle had been bedding down here, so the brush was gone and the lower twigs broken off the trees. I went through fast to cover the way I had come. But when the rider appeared he was lower down, about where I had gone into the aspens.

I didn't want to kill a good horse so I shot high, aiming for his shoulders. The shot hit him as I saw him jerk in the saddle and then he was off, running.

For a few minutes I sat easy, listening and waiting. I wasn't wishful of killing folks, and here lately the laws had been tightenin' up. This was the 1880s and folks didn't look kindly on killings. I had no wish to tangle with the law in a country where I was a stranger. The sore spots on my neck were just healed and were still tender.

Finally I came out of the woods after scouting my horse, then when I saw it was safe I came out, mounted up, and started back to the ranch, cutting across country. Twice I startled deer.

It was a time to be careful. I walked the roan, keeping under cover when possible, checking my back trail and around the country. The only part that worried me was the ridge. If somebody got up there I'd be a wide-open target, so I scanned the ridge, time to time. When I came down to the ranch it was from behind the big barn. Dismounting, I shifted my riggin' to the buckskin and turned the roan into the corral. Keeping my rifle, I walked back to the granary, glancing toward the house. Nobody was in sight, so I opened the granary door and pushed it wider with the muzzle of my rifle. I am not what you'd call a trusting man and had no idea who might have been here since I left.

Everything seemed just as I'd left it. What gear I had I put together, although it wasn't much. Then I sat down on the bed to think.

That will I'd found worried me. Mrs. Hollyrood had gone to the law with Phillips' will and they had accepted it. No doubt it was later than this one, although from the date it could not have been much later.

Why would a man who left everything to his "beloved niece" completely disown her in another will? And where was that niece? Had Phillips ever spoken of her to Mrs. Hollyrood?

Now I was no lawyer, and knew too little of such things, but I had a hunch that the will I had was important and should be submitted to the court. But why? Phillips had written another will, had given everything to Mrs. Hollyrood, and that was all there was to it. Nobody seemed to have made any protest but Lew Paine and for him I had no sympathy. If he felt she was wrongfully in possession he should have gone to the law. This country was changing. The old rough stuff didn't go anymore.

It disappointed me that Mrs. Hollyrood was thinking of selling the place. It was too good a ranch, and one with a lot of free land around for grazing. Most of the time she wouldn't need more than one hand, so it would be cheap to operate.

Those men who attacked me today, one at least had been one of Lew Paine's men. I'd shot to put them out of action, so was hoping I'd killed nobody. That last man, however, about him I wasn't sure. One thing was a cinch. They'd be careful next time. If there was a next time. I was going to light a shuck.

Nobody around here knew me, and anybody I had trouble with would have friends. Mrs. Hollyrood was pulling out and I'd no reason to stay on, so every bit of common sense I had warned me to ride out and ride fast.

Lew Paine and his boys or the Burrows outfit might want my hide stretched, but I had nothing against them. All I wanted was to be alone in the mountains, hunting a little, prospecting a mite, and just generally enjoying the country. Somewhere in my breeding there must have been a bighorn sheep because I surely did like the high-up country with the clouds for company.

First, I wanted a bill of sale on the blue roan. I'd buy the horse if they wouldn't give it to me like they'd said, and then I'd ride over to Parrott City and get myself some grub. After restin' up a mite I'd leave out of here at night and go back to pick up my horses and gear. That ride would take me all of three or four days but I'd travel by night, and ride into town in the night, too. I wanted no trouble.

There was a lamp lighted in the house now. Suddenly I wasn't anxious to go in, but I dearly wanted the roan and was afraid somebody would shoot it if I didn't ride out of here with it.

So I combed my hair, washed my hands, and went across the road to the house and rapped on the door, then stepped in like I'd been doing.

Matty was at the stove. "Sit down," she said, "I'll have it on in a minute."

"Mrs. Hollyrood around? I thought we might close the deal on that roan. Nobody seems to want the horse and she said I could have it."

"She will be out soon." Matty didn't look around at me. "She's had a lot to think about."

"If she sells out, I'd not like to have that horse go with the outfit. Lew Paine was fixin' to kill it."

"You'll have to admit the horse has a bad reputation," Matty said, "but I'd hate to see it killed."

"That Pinkerton is still around. He was camped about a half-mile up the road."

Matty had no comment and in a. moment she was putting food before me, then she brought her own plate and sat down across from me. She glanced toward the inner door, then said quietly, "I thought you'd be leaving."

"Yes, ma'am. I wanted a bill of sale for the roan." Did she want me to go? Why had she advised it? I looked at her again. I had never seen a woman so beautiful, with such a calm, still face. Only her eyes seemed to move or show expression, and now, I wonder I hadn't seen it before, she looked haunted.

"What is that Pinkerton man's name? Have you heard?"

"Told me hisself. He's Reed Bell."

The name seemed to mean nothing to her. "I wonder why he stays around? Is he so sure the person he wants is around here?"

I shrugged. "Maybe he likes the country. He's got himself a right nice camp, only he should watch himself. There's bears on the mountain above him. Tracks all over the place."

She was right behind me before I realized. I smelled her before I heard her, she moved that quiet. But that perfume she wore, it was a wonderful smell.

"Did you finish with your counting of cattle?" she asked, sitting down at the head of the table between us.

"Just about. I figure there's about seven hundred head on the place and that agrees with Phillips' tally. There's prob'ly a few drifted over in Spring Gulch or out east or west of here. Even when the grazin' is good there's always a few will wander off."

"Have you found a buyer for me?"

"Haven't had a chance. Today I had a run-in with some of Lew Paine's boys. You must have heard the shooting."

"I did." She glanced at me. "You seem to have come out of it pretty well."

"They ran into trouble," I agreed. Changing the subject, I said, "I was wonderin' about the blue roan?"

"The Death Horse?" She looked at me. "I think you should have it." She looked over at Matty. "Will you give me the paper? And the pen and inkwell."

She took a piece of paper and wrote out a bill of sale for me. "There! The roan horse is yours, and you've earned it." She turned her eyes to me. "You are leaving?"

"Well, I've my gear and two horses up the country a piece. I thought I'd go get them, then stop back here for a day or two before I light out." I wasn't at all sure that once away I'd ever come back, but had an idea it was better to let her think that. Besides, I might just come back. I surely do hate to leave things half-done, and there were things here needed doin'.

"My idea was to leave here at night so's Lew Paine an' them wouldn't know I was gone."

"That is very thoughtful of you, but Mr. Paine does not

worry me. In fact, I have been thinking of having a talk with him. Maybe if we talked he would see the error of his ways."

She changed the subject then and began to talk of the theater and of plays she'd been in like *East Lynne* and *Lady of Lyons*. It was mighty pleasant, sitting there in the soft light of the coal-oil lamps, with the smell of fresh coffee in the room, hearing her tell stories of that life so far from this.

"We had our troubles, too," she added. "Once when we were playing a small town on the Mississippi several men tried to break up the show. One of our men stopped it, but there was some shooting."

"Three of them? He must've been good."

"Parmalee Sackett? He was very skillful with a gun. I'd heard that he'd shot a riverboat gambler before he joined the company." She paused. "He really wasn't an actor but he did very well and could have made a career of it."

"What happened to him?" I was curious.

"Something happened out west. He left us very suddenly, in fact. I believe some relative of his was in trouble, but that was many years ago."

Goin' to plays an' such was something I'd never done much of, although here and there, in Tombstone or Deadwood, they had theaters puttin' on plays. I seen a play once in Denver, too. I mentioned that.

"Denver?" Her voice was a little higher. "I never had the opportunity to play there."

"Wasn't that where Mr. Phillips died?"

"Yes, yes, it was. My company had gone back east, however."

Folding the bill of sale, I put it in my shirt pocket. "I'd better get some rest."

"You sure you don't want to buy the ranch, Mr. Passin'?"

"Me? I ain't got that much. I'd have to strike another rich pocket before I could afford a ranch."

"Every little bit helps, though, Mr. Passin'. That's what I always say, every little bit helps. Now don't you forget"—she arose and gathered her robe about her—"when you come back by I want to fix you a nice supper, something really nice. You've been very kind."

"Yes, ma'am."

Outside in the night I mopped my forehead and wondered why I was sweating. It was cool out here and it had not been that warm inside.

I was riding west, all right, and I'd pick up my horses and come back through here. Maybe I'd stop over, but somehow I had a hunch that nice supper she planned to fix for me, somehow I didn't feel I'd ever get to eat that meal.

Maybe it was just a hunch, and maybe something more.

ELEVEN

The way prices were these days I might have bought the ranch, but probably not. Lots of land was free for the taking. A man could homestead a place, and if he settled on a water hole he'd control the range all around. Grass was no good without water.

Right now I had more money than ever in my life before. I had twelve hundred and forty-six dollars. That was what I'd taken from that pocket I discovered, and besides that I had twenty-eight dollars of walking-around money. That is, I had that twenty-eight dollars when I found the pocket for spending along the way. The twelve hundred and forty-six was my stake, and right now I was going to head for the high-up hills, find myself a little camp, and contemplate.

I mean I had to think what I was going to do. When a man has always worked for the other fellow and never had more than his wages, that twelve hundred and forty-six dollars was a lot of money.

I was born poor and raised poor, and my pa was a hardworkin' man who always gave a day's work for a day's pay, the same as me. He never saw this much money in his whole life, I suspect, and I'd never had so much or even seen that much in any place but a gamblin' house. So I needed to contemplate.

Nobody needed to tell me I might never have so much again, although a man is always wishful about it. I'd never been a hand for whiskey. Oh, I took a drink now and again but had never been drunk in my life and never wanted to be. I always figured if I had my wits about me I could figure my way out of any corner I might get into, but a man drinking . . . well, his judgment's not that good, although he thinks it is.

Take Houston Burrows, now. He'd been drinking and now he was dead. Had he been sober he might have been a shade more cautious with a man he'd never seen before. Not that he would have been any luckier. He just wasn't anywhere near as good with a gun as he thought. It's easy to be a giant when you are walking among pygmies.

As for gamblin', I knew too much about it. I just left that to others, so I wasn't about to lose my money to some card mechanic or roulette wheel. Nor was I going to drink it up. All my life I'd worked for wages, except when prospectin', and never had more than thirty dollars a month. Now I had to get myself alone up above the aspen somewhere and just look out over a lot of country and think.

The work I'd done around the ranch, well, the roan was ample payment for that. I might have done it anyway, as those womenfolks were alone there and I just hate to see a place all run down like that. When I seen a load that needed to be carried it was just my nature to back up to it and carry it where it needed to be. That was the way with that ranch. I rode in there and saw that gate hanging on a broken hinge, saw broken rails and holes needed patchin' an' fence posts leanin' ever' which way . . . well, I just had to fix it up. I just don't know no better.

Folks have called me a hard man. It's just that I don't take to bein' pushed. Like that Burrows, now, I had nothing against him but I just hate to get shot.

Lead lies heavy on the stomach and a man can digest only so much of it. All I wanted that night was a drink to cut the dust out of my throat, then a meal and a bed. Killing a man is nothing to be proud of, even if the man is armed and coming at you. If it has to be done, you do it.

The granary was dark. I lighted the old lantern I had and looked around, then put the light out and undressed in the dark, not being a trusting man. Before I got into bed I pulled the latch string inside so nobody could open the door whilst I was sleeping.

Lying back on the bed with my hands clasped behind my head, I tried to think about the situation. What I should do was to take that will to a judge somewhere and leave it with him to do what he was of a mind to. Then I'd ride off down the trail.

The trouble with my trying to think of a nighttime is that whilst my intentions are good I always fall asleep. So when daybreak came I was no further along. I just saddled up the buckskin and took the trail to Parrott City. Only I didn't follow the trail. I just didn't want to be anywhere I might be expected to be.

Parrott City was warm in the sunshine when I rode into town, and I tied the buckskin and went to an eating joint. It was better than when I was there before, with red-and-white checkered tablecloths and even curtains in the windows. A man and his wife were running the place and they set a good table. And that was just what it was, two long tables with benches on either side.

I picked a place where I could watch the door and ordered breakfast. Looking at the grub they put before me, they must have figured I was a whole roundup crew, but it was remarkable what I did to it.

When I had surrounded and destroyed about half of what they put before me the door opened and that girl came in. She came in, and as I was the only person eating she came right over to me.

"Are you riding that buckskin?"

"No, ma'am. I'm eatin' breakfast. Will you join me?"

"Did you ride that buckskin to town?"

"It was either that or walk and I never walk anywhere when I can get a horseback."

She was a right pretty girl and was the one I'd seen in town before. I had stood up when she spoke to me and now I said, "Ma'am? Won't you sit down? I can't sit whilst you're standin' an' my breakfast is gettin' cold."

She sat down, and I did, too. The woman who ran the place along with her husband, she came out and brought coffee. "Breakfast, miss?"

"No, thank you. I've already eaten."

She looked at me out of the prettiest blue eyes I'd seen in a month of Sundays and she said, "That horse belongs to me."

"He's a fine horse," I said.

"Is that all you have to say?"

"No, ma'am. Time to time I talk right smart. As a matter of fact I just rode him over from the ranch. I was figurin' on breakfast and maybe seein' you."

"Me?"

"Yes, ma'am. I saw you over here just the other day, and I thought then I'd surely like to see you again. I hadn't tried because I'm not much of a hand with women. I can handle a horse or cow, a pick or shovel, a single jack and drill steel, or a gun, but with women I don't do so good. Especially when they are as pretty as you."

"You're doing all right."

"Thank you, ma'am. I had an idea who you were. You're Janet Le Caudy."

Her eyes were cool. "Now how did you know that?"

"I got a mule that reads the past, present, and future," I said. "He told me who you were and that you owned half the ranch I've been workin' on."

She looked at me, a faint stir of amusement in her eyes. "I'd like to meet your mule. What else did he tell you?"

"That you had best be very careful around here. Several other people claim that ranch and one of them is Lew Paine."

"He's a relative by marriage but I've never met him."

"You're lucky. If I were you I'd avoid him."

"Do you work for that woman? The one who is living on the ranch?"

"There's two women. No, I don't exactly work for them although I've been fixin' up around. Do you know Reed Bell?"

"No, I don't believe I do."

"Kind of a square-built man? Wearin' city clothes? A brown suit, often. Thick mustache?"

"I've seen him around town."

"He's a Pink. I mean, a Pinkerton man, a detective."

"So?"

"He's lookin' for some woman, a young woman."

"And you believe it might be me?"

"No, ma'am." I was embarrassed. "This woman would be about thirty, maybe thirty-five. You can't be more than twenty."

"I am nineteen, and I assure you, I haven't murdered anyone."

The woman came in and filled my cup. Janet Le Caudy looked up. "I believe I'll have a cup, too."

When she had her coffee and a swallow of it I said, "Ma'am? Being as you're part owner of that ranch, I'd like to clear something with you. There's a blue roan—"

"The Death Horse?"

I winced a mite. "Ma'am, others may call him that. I like that horse, and for work I've done about the place Mrs. Hollyrood gave me a bill of sale for the roan. Bein' you're half-owner, that bill of sale might not carry me far if you weren't happy with it.

If that horse is left around here, somebody is goin' to shoot him. Lew Paine was about to when I stopped him. That's a fine animal, ma'am, an' we like each other. Maybe it's because he's a loner like me."

"He is said to be a jinx." She studied me, and I saw her eyes go to my open shirt where the red scars of the rope burn still showed. "Aren't you afraid?"

"No, ma'am. That horse brought me to where you are."

She looked at me again, her eyes level and cool, but she seemed to ignore what I'd said. "Those women at the ranch? What are they like?"

Well, now? What were they like? I mulled that one over a mite. "Mrs. Hollyrood, she's an actress. Matty was with the show for a time, too, but I reckon she's new at it. Both of them conduct themselves like ladies. I never saw them anyplace but in the ranch house, and Mrs. Hollyrood—"

"Does she have a good figure?"

That embarrassed me a mite and Janet Le Caudy saw it. You see, I wasn't accustomed to talkin' about women's shapes, not with other women, at least. "I don't rightly know. She always wears a robe. You know, like a kimono or something. My guess would be"—and this was something I hadn't thought of before— "that she has a good figure."

"Gray hair, you said?"

"Yes, ma'am, but always beautifully combed. She keeps herself well and she's a handsome woman."

"Always combed?"

"Yes, ma'am, like she'd stepped out of a bandbox, as the saying is."

"And Matty?"

"A rarely beautiful young woman. Very cool. Smiles almost none at all. Only feature seems to move is her eyes, but I got an idea she listens, too. There's no scare in her. When one of Paine's friends rushed the house with a torch to burn them out, she shot him dead."

"Good for her. That's a beautifully built house. I'd not like to see it burned."

"She didn't waste no time. She just didn't say aye, yes, or no, she just threw down on him and she wasn't intending to miss."

"What did Mrs. Hollyrood say to that?"

"She never commented on it."

We sat quiet. Looking out the door I could see the shape of the mountain called Baldy, just opposite, beyond the trail that led up La Plata Canyon. The sky was marvelously blue, scattered with white clouds.

"They're planning to sell the ranch," I said.

She smiled. "They will find themselves in trouble. That ranch is almost all I have in the world, and I want it." She looked at me. "I want all of it. Uncle John wanted me to have it. He told me so several times."

"He told you so?"

"I have several letters he wrote to me."

And in my pocket I had a will that left it all to her. This shaped up like a women's fight and I couldn't see any way I could get anything but the worst of it because I stood right in the middle of it. All my good sense told me to get that roan and light out. I mean, to put some trail behind me. But that would mean I would have to leave where she was.

That stopped me cold in my thinkin' tracks. Was I off my trail completely? All the sign showed trouble comin' and trouble that was none of mine. Was I going to get myself shot over a pair of blue eyes and some freckles across her nose? And what about Matty? Or Mrs. Hollyrood, who was plannin' on fixin' supper for me?

Settin' there across the table from her, I found myself not wantin' to pick up an' move. All my life I'd had trouble talkin' to womenfolks but I had no such trouble with her. Moreover, she was in trouble. But so were those other women, so just where did I stand? I had a will, but I had no idea what it meant. If Phillips had written a later will, this here one I had wasn't worth the paper it was written on.

"Ma'am? Was I you I'd walk careful. I don't have any idea what you're up against but I've a feelin' these folks can be right mean. That Lew Paine, now—"

"I know about him." She looked up at me. "I have a friend, too, a man who has offered to help me. He knows about situations and people like these. He should ride into town almost anytime now."

"An old friend?"

"No, as a matter of fact, I just met him. When he found out where I was going, he became interested, he said he had property out here and would help me. He thinks I should meet with Mrs. Hollyrood and settle it out of court. He suggested I ride out to the ranch with him."

Well, I got my back up. Was I jealous? What right had I to be? Nonetheless, I was suspicious. These strangers a person meets traveling . . . well, a body has to be careful.

"I'll be around," I said. "If you need me, call on me." Suddenly, I was even more suspicious. "This man you met? Is he a lawyer?"

"He's an Englishman. He is an adjuster for some estates in England and is accustomed to dealing with matters of this kind."

"Their laws are different than ours." Were my suspicions due to jealousy?

"He's a very distinguished man. His name is Charles Pelham Clinton, and he said he would be glad to speak for me. He has to be here anyway."

Well, maybe. But I made a vow to be around and keep my eyes open. Still, I admitted grudgingly, it could happen just that way. She was a mighty fetching girl, and a man who had to be here anyway— Well, why not? I'd have done it. In fact, I was offering to do what I could.

We talked some more and then she suddenly got up. "I must be going, Mister—?"

"They been callin' me Mr. Passin', for Passin' Through, which I usually am."

"All right, Mr. Passin', and thank you for your offer of help. I doubt if I shall need it, but thank you, anyway."

"About that blue roan—"

"Later. We will discuss that later."

With that, she was gone. I paid for my meal, and as the woman was gatherin' the dishes I asked her, "That Englishman? Has he been in here?"

"Mr. Clinton? Oh, yes, indeed! A very handsome gentleman he is, too! And such nice manners!"

Feeling no better, I walked out on the street, tightened the cinch a little, and studied about the situation. It seems I was out of it all around. Mrs. Hollyrood surely didn't need me any longer, and Janet Le Caudy didn't either.

If I just had clear title to that blue roan I'd saddle up and ride off down the trail and leave them to settle their own affairs. Reed Bell didn't seem to be anywhere around so I mounted up and headed out of town.

Just as I started into the trees, a spanking-new rig, all shining and beautiful, came down the trail with a man in a white suit driving. He wore a picturesque white hat and handled the lines like an expert.

That was him! I just knew it was him. It was that Englishman, and there couldn't be two like that in the country.

He was a handsome man with a neatly trimmed blond mustache, and a shotgun beside him leaning against the seat.

Charles Pelham Clinton. It was a name I'd not forget.

TWELVE

When I rode down through the pines to where I could look across the creek at the ranch, I drew rein. It was a magnificent sweep of country. The ranch lay at the foot of a ridge about two miles long ending in what folks around here called Maggie's Rock. Aside from the meadows the place was pretty well covered with Gambel oak or ponderosa pine, while in the folds of the ridge aspen trailed down toward the meadows.

At the far end from Maggie's Rock there was another high point, and below it the thick stand of aspen where I'd ridden before. It was a beautiful place, and whoever the owner was, they had my envy. It was enough to stop a man from wandering.

Under cover of the trees I studied the layout, carefully examining each clump of trees, each approach. These were uneasy days, for enemies might be awaiting me behind any rock or bush. I looked to see how the shadows fell, how the birds flew, and where the deer fed. Each might give an indication of where an enemy was or wasn't.

Finally, I walked the buckskin down the draw back of the house, drawing up when I came in sight. Something was worrying my mind and I didn't know what. Finally I turned my horse and rode along the low ridge back of the house, keeping out of sight over the ridge, and came down to the trail well past the house, riding back to the granary from the west.

It was past midday and I switched my saddle to the roan, then went up the house. When I rapped, there was no response. Puzzled, I knocked again, thinking I heard stirrings within. Or was it my imagination?

When I rapped again and there was no answer I turned the knob and entered. The kitchen was empty and still. There was

80

a tablet on the table where somebody had been writin', I could see the faint indentations left by a pencil. Without thinking much of why, I tored off the top sheet and folded it into my pocket. Then I wrote a couple of lines telling them I was going after my horses, and signed it *Passin'*.

There was a faint movement behind me and I turned. Mrs. Hollyrood stood in the doorway, wearing that robe, her gray hair just as neatly dressed as ever, but the look in her eyes was cold.

"What are you doing here?"

"Came back to switch horses, ma'am. Thought I'd leave you a note explainin' where I'm goin' an' when I'll be back. I didn't wish for you to think I'd just run out on you."

"Yes, of course. I am sorry, but I heard the movement out here and was frightened."

Maybe . . . but she sure hadn't looked frightened.

For some reason she was different, and she even looked different. "You were in Parrott City?"

"Yes, ma'am. It ain't much of a place, you know. Just a few hundred people around and most of them are workin' in mines or are prospectin'. There's an eatin' place, what they call a hotel, and a couple of supply stores an' saloons.

"I did hear folks talkin' an' the railroad is into a place they call Durango. It's near Animas City. You were talkin' of goin' east. You could catch the steam cars there, I reckon. Although you could probably catch the train this side of there. I've seen the rails but I don't know where they've built a station, or if they have."

She still stood in the doorway to her bedroom. Pickin' up the note I'd written, I said something about her not needing it now. "I'll be gone four, five days. Maybe less. I'll come by this way and if there's anything I can do for you—"

"Thank you, and you must let me fix supper for you before you go. You've been very helpful, you know."

"Thank you, ma'am." With that I stepped outside and for some reason I was sweating. Walking over to the roan I said, "You an' me, we're gettin' out of here."

I'd like to have said goodbye to Matty. Where was she? She was the one I'd have expected to come out, but there'd been no sign of her.

Mornin' would have been the proper time to ride out on a trip like this but I just wanted to get shut of the place and get out on the trail where my thoughts could work. Most of my serious thinkin', if you could call it that, was done in the saddle. Out ridin' alone gave a man a chance to sort out his thoughts when he was not bothered by other folks bein' around or other things to watch and consider.

"We're goin' back," I said to the roan, "an' I hope we're not ridin' into trouble, but I've gear over yonder that I want, and things I'll need, so we'll just go fetch them."

That night, ten miles west of the ranch, I camped behind a small grove of trees near a stream. Off to the northeast were the Rampart Hills, and westward the range called the Sleeping Ute lay along the skyline, looking like a huge Indian lying on his back, his arms folded across his chest. Mesa Verde, where there were said to be ancient rock-built cities hidden in the canyons, lay just a mite further west.

Before day broke I was in the saddle, pushing on toward the west.

The first thing I saw were fresh tracks, made the night before. Four riders, heading west at a trot. They were traveling after I camped so they must have bedded down somewhere up ahead and not too far off. Swinging off the trail, I kept to low ground, but near Mud Creek their tracks veered off to the north. Looked to me they were going to camp in that same cave I'd camped when ridin' east, the one some folks called the Cowboy Hotel, on account so many stopped there.

Now those four riders might be strangers on their own business but I was taking no chances. It could just be Lew Paine or some of the Burrows outfit.

Three days later, with it coming up to darkness, I skirted the town where I'd left my stock. Waiting outside until most folks would be at supper, I rode through the back streets up to the livery stable.

Now I knew I was riding a known horse, and one folks would be sure to comment on if they saw it, so I tied him to the corral back of the stable and walked through from the back end. It had big wide-open doors at each end so I could see right through to the street.

The hostler was sitting in a chair by the front opening and he saw me coming right off but just kept to his chair and waited. He was an old-timer with gray hair and a handlebar mustache and he looked like he'd been up the creek and over the mountain.

"You still holdin' my horses?"

He tipped back in his chair and gave me a quizzical look out of blue eyes that had seen a lot of country. "Yep, kep' 'em in good shape. Figured you'd be back."

"I left some duffle, too. Stowed in the tack room."

"It's there. I seen it, left it alone, and said nothing."

Going into the tack room, I picked up my gear and carried it out, then saddled up my own horse and the packhorse as well. When I had the pack in place I led the horses out back and tied them with the roan. I now had two saddled horses, two rifles, and ammunition enough to fight a war. Also, in the gear loaded on the packhorse was my pick, shovel, and ax.

"Better keep a lookout, there's some boys in town look like they were huntin' somebody."

"Some of the Burrows outfit?"

"Two of them rode in." He looked up at me from under those thick brows. "There's three more in town, and there were two other fellers with them who rode in. I'd say they knew you were comin'."

"How much do I owe you?"

"I'd call it even for twenty dollars. I grained your horses a couple of times. Figured when you needed them you'd need them bad."

"Thanks. I'll need them tonight."

"You ridin' out now?"

"No." I paused a minute. "I never finished that drink I ordered over yonder in the saloon. I reckon I'll go over an' get it."

"They'll be there."

"I know it, but I'd rather get it over with than have them hangin' on my trail."

"Well, it's your funeral. I never cottoned to Houston Burrows. When you shot him you done the town a favor, but you pay some mind to a stocky-built man, about forty-odd, about five foot nine. His name is Dave Swain and he runs with the Burrows outfit. He's an eastern man who come west an' dug in. He's mean as all get-out, so don't you take him light."

"Is there a side door or back door?"

"Both. Better you should take the side door. She lets you in right at the end of the bar."

"I remember it now. All right. If I don't come back you can keep my outfit."

"I'd rather see you come back. I never liked any of that outfit. Ever' once in a while I feel like gettin' down my old Sharps an' givin' them what for, but I'm gettin' old, I reckon, an' they ain't bothered me except by secondhand."

He paused. "You want some backup?"

"No, thanks. This is one I've got to do for myself and somebody else, also."

So I slipped the thong off my six-shooter and went across the street and into the side door.

There were eight or ten men at the bar, a card table goin', and several standers-around. I walked up to the end of the bar but they were busy talking and paid me no mind. The bartender saw me and turned a couple of shades of gray, gray, and grayer. He came down the bar and started to speak. "I came back to finish my drink," I said. "Put it on the bar."

"They'll kill you!" His voice was hoarse. "For God's sake, man, get—!"

They turned around. I'd already picked out Dave Swain. I remembered him from the lynchin' party, soon as ever I saw him. Bob Burrows was there, and Andy, too. I'd picked up their names from listenin' around.

"Howdy," I said. "Seems like we've met before."

Well, they didn't know what to say. They'd wanted to kill me and some of them had made a try at it, but here I was, right in their home camp, but it was one thing when you shoot at somebody from ambush and something else when you face him at point-blank range, and some of them had seen me kill Houston Burrows, who was their ring-tailed terror.

"You must be crazy!" Bob Burrows said.

"I come by to pick up some horses. You boys seemed to be goin' out of your way to hunt me so I figured I'd save you time an' trouble."

Nobody moved. One man sort of licked his upper lip, another sort of turned his face away, not looking at me. Swain was at a table, to one side.

The bartender put my drink on the bar and I put down a two-bit piece. "Keep it," the bartender said, "an' drink up. An' please, mister, don't shoot nobody in here! I just mopped the floor!"

This was a bunch I didn't like, and whilst I wanted no trouble I didn't want to spend my days watching my back trail for a bunch of dry-gulchers. If it had to happen, this was as good a place as any.

Swain was lookin' at me, a hard, amused look in his eyes. He was a dangerous man. The rest of them were a bunch of loudmouthed four-flushers.

I took half my drink and put the glass down. My attention was on them all, pointing a direct challenge at none of them. When you meet a man's eyes he often thinks it's a challenge, and I didn't want a shooting if it could be avoided.

At the same time, I wanted them to know I was ready, so maybe they'd back off and leave me alone. Nobody said anything so I finished my drink, leaving my two bits on the bar. I didn't want something for nothing.

"Some of you," I said, "were here when Houston Burrows picked his fight. All I wanted was a drink, a meal, and to ride on. He wanted to show how mean he was. If you want to know, he wasn't even medium fast. He couldn't even walk the trails with men like Langford Peel, Bill Tilghman, Dave Masters, or Luke Short."

"Who *are* you, mister?"

The man who asked it was sitting at a table near Swain. He was an older man, wearing a beat-up suit and a derby hat.

"They call me Passin' Through," I said, "because that's what I'm usually doin', especially now." I straightened up from the bar. "I came back to pick up my outfit. I don't have no quarrel with you boys, an' I had none with Houston Burrows. He just swung too wide a loop."

"He was a damned good man!" Bob Burrows spoke angrily, defensively.

"In Dodge or Deadwood they'd have had him sweepin' the floors," I said. "You boys ride your trail an' I'll ride mine, but the fun's over. If I find anybody ridin' up behind me it's open season."

For the first time I saw a tall, lean man sittin' back against the wall. I'd never seen him before but right off I knew who he was and I felt my scalp crawl. The door was only three steps behind me, so when I'd stepped back from the bar it was down to two steps. I took another step backward, then went sidewise through the door, not forgetting there might be somebody waiting outside. There wasn't.

The street was empty and still. There were only nine or ten buildings along the street and a scattering of houses and shacks

behind them. Lights showed through the canvas of a couple of
tents. Nothing moved, anywhere. Waiting for just a minute
and listening for the slightest sound, say of somebody going out
a back door, I crossed to the livery stable.

The hostler was at the door. "Didn't hear any shootin'."

"They didn't make an issue of it. I had my drink, now I'm
putting this country behind me. Thanks, friend. It's been a
pleasure."

"If you come by again, stop in. Enjoy havin' a drink with
you." He paused. "You see anybody in there you knew?"

Only four buildings along the street were lighted, but nothing moved in front of the windows. A cool wind, very soft,
brought the smell of pines from the mountains. It was a good
country, a wonderful country, too good to let the likes of them
spoil it. But they were just would-be toughs, they'd swing their
shoulders around, glower a little, and create a few problems,
but before long they'd all be pushin' up daisies out on Boot Hill
and nobody would even remember them.

"Yeah," I said, "I saw one man I hadn't seen around before."

"Figured you'd see him. Rode in a couple of days ago. He's
just been sort of lookin' around."

"He with them?"

"Knows 'em. Or does now. They ain't got that kind of money
an' wouldn't spend it for killin' if they had it." The old hostler
paused. "His kind come high. Either somebody has money to
spend or he owes somebody a favor." He looked up at me.
"That could be it."

Mounting the Appaloosa to give the roan a rest, I led the
other two down the alleys and back streets, past some ram-
shackle barns and sheds as well as a pretty little house with a
white picket fence and a light in the window and down into a
sandy wash that ran alongside the trail.

A mile out of town I rode up on the trail and drew rein to
listen. Sitting there in the cool night I looked back at a town
that had never welcomed me, but looked at it with regret.
Folks were living there, folks I would never know, each finding
happiness or hoping for it, and each in his or her own way. I
liked seeing the lights in the windows. Only a few years back
there weren't any lights or windows to shine from or folks to
light them. A lot of people had come from a lot of places, but to
each one his home was the end of a trail that started somewhere afar off.

I'd ride back to the ranch, say my goodbyes, and maybe even accept that supper Mrs. Hollyrood had offered to fix for me. Then I would reach for the high-up hills and let them worry about their problems without me. Looked like I was getting involved, and I didn't want that, yet it was irritating because of all the loose ends.

Who rightly owned the ranch? Had Phillips actually written a second will that left his "beloved niece" out of it? Without explanation? It didn't make sense. And who had hired Pan Beacham, and for what?

Who in all that crowd could afford him? Pan was a sure-thing killer for hire, known as such but never caught in the act, never arrested. An even thousand dollars was his reputed price, and that was a lot of money.

Had somebody hired Pan Beacham to kill me?

THIRTEEN

He had sat back there watching, saying nothing, making no move, just watching, and he had been watching me. Beacham was like that. By the time he made his move he knew what he was going to do and how, but I knew he liked to have a line on those he was to kill. He wanted to know them, to understand them, to know what he might expect.

Chances were that I knew more of Beacham than he knew of me. That "Passin' Through" business wouldn't mean anything to him. He would be trying to sort me out, if he didn't already know, to decide who I was and why. If it was me he was gunning for. And if it was, who hired him? Who would want me dead that much?

There were people who would like to see me lying dead but most of them were cheapskates. If they couldn't do it themselves they'd never dream of paying anybody to do it for them.

Somebody either had money to spend or Beacham owed somebody a favor.

Amongst some trees on a low knoll back from the trail I made a late, cold camp. If by some chance Pan Beacham was followin' me, I wasn't goin' to send up a smoke to bring him to me. Picketing my horses on the grass inside the cluster of trees, I bedded down in the shadows and slept, trusting my horses would warn me.

An hour before daylight I came down from the trees and headed east.

For a man wary of trouble I'd picked up a lot of people who were huntin' my hide, and when I rode out that morning I had a nasty feelin'. Trouble was riding my way and I'd best get set

88

for it. I shucked my rifle and checked the loads, though I didn't need to. I held that rifle in my hands.

Did they know I had three horses? I doubted it. Beacham might, for he'd be checking around, making sure of things. Suddenly I left the trail and rode up into the trees. For a few minutes I sat my horse, studying the country around. Keeping under cover was not going to be easy, and those hunting me might know the country better than I.

My fingers rubbed the stubble on my jaw. Before I saw any womenfolk I was going to have to shave. Nothing moved back along the trail, nor in the country around. So why was I jumpy? And I was. I wiped my hands on my shirtfront and squinted, looking over the sunlit land before me.

Riding out of the trees, I kept to low ground, skirting the base of a tree-clad ridge. Suddenly, I pulled up, listening. I'd heard a horse running, or was I imagining it?

My eyes swept the country again. There was no dust, but there wouldn't be in this grass-covered country. The valley was wide, broken by occasional low ridges and knolls, mostly fringed with trees. There were a couple of small streams. Wary of open country, I headed back into the trees, working my way toward higher country.

Abruptly, I turned at right angles to the route I'd been following and dipped deeper into the trees, seeking open areas in the woods or game trails.

Slowly I worked my way through the trees, across open glades abloom with wildflowers, into the shadowed forest again, pausing now and again to listen. There was just no way I could travel with three horses in this kind of country and not leave a trail, and I had to ride wary for more reason than them who followed, for I did not know the country and did not want to be trapped in a cul-de-sac somewhere.

Swinging wide to avoid a patch of thistles, I glimpsed an opening in the forest and looked down where I'd been traveling. As I looked, four riders came into sight, one of them riding a horse Lew Paine rode. It was probably him.

They pulled up, looking along the mountain ahead of me. One of them pointed toward something and they started toward it.

Not hesitating, I started down the side of the hill toward

them. By the time I reached the edge of the woods they were gone, so I crossed their trail and headed south and away from them.

By noontime I was butting up against the west side of a towering mesa split with canyons, all pointing their fingers at me as if beckoning. As I wasn't hunting a fight, I headed that way and stumbled on a trail, it was a dim trail, not traveled much, but I was in no position to be choosy.

It was slow going, and the worst of it was if anybody looked back that way they might glimpse me from time to time. In my favor was the fact that they'd never expect me to be going where I was.

The trail switched back and forth a couple of times, working its way up the steep side. Not knowing this country well, I could just guess that I was climbing the north rim of Mesa Verde, but it might be another mesa further west.

Standing among the cedars atop the ridge, I studied my back trail. There was no sign of movement, and if my luck held they would be looking for me off to the east where I should have been. From where I stood I could see for miles.

Far off to the northwest were the Abajo Mountains and beyond them the La Sals, where I'd been not long since. The air was clear, with no smoke, and only a few high clouds. Off to the south I could see the high pinnacle of Shiprock, down New Mexico way. Again I looked back the way I had come and saw no movement, so went back into the cedar near the fallen rocks of a ruined building, and made my camp. This time I was far enough away and back in the cedars so I built a fire.

There was some graze for the stock, so I picketed the horses. The long-ago Indians who built this place had also put a wall across a natural run-off spot and trapped water from the recent rains. There was enough for me and for the horses and maybe a bit more.

Whilst I was building my fire a coyote came for water. Unused to people, he was also unafraid and came to within fifty feet of my camp.

He drank, looked over at me, then watching me from the corners of his eyes he drank again, looked at me with his head up and one paw raised, then trotted away, figuring I was of no account. Getting bacon out of my pack, I fried myself a bait and made frying-pan bread. It was getting on to sundown, and even if they found my trail again they'd probably not try that trail in the dark, not knowing where I'd be.

Setting by my small fire, drinking the coffee I'd been wanting, I speculated about the women at the ranch.

Mrs. Hollyrood now, she never seemed to go anywhere. Not that Parrott City or Animas City had much to offer, but womenfolks always like to shop around and look things over. She never left the ranch. Of course, bein' an actress an' all she'd probably had her fill of travel.

She was a right handsome woman, her beautiful gray hair always perfectly done, and few wrinkles for a woman her age.

Matty now, Matty was what some folks, like that English lord I guided, they would call her beauty classical. She was perfectly beautiful and beautifully perfect, if you get what I mean. Only she never seemed to smile. Her only expression was in her eyes.

Just who was she? There had been nothing wrong with her shooting when she shot that man riding at her with a torch. She'd grown up shooting, of course, but most folks would show more feeling, it seemed to me. She shot that man because she had it to do and that was all there was to it.

In my pocket I had the will that said Janet Le Caudy was to inherit the ranch, and when I got back, something would have to be done about that. And I was on my way back.

Yet, when I took a last look around, walking to the cliff edge and listening, it was Janet I was thinking about. "Le Caudy" sounded like Bill Cody's name, but the way she spelled it was French, I guess. A mighty pretty woman.

My fire was dying but the coffee was still hot. I drank another cup and then stretched out on my bed and slept like a baby.

Twice during the night I awakened, listened into the night, and once I walked to the cliff edge. The stars were bright in the sky, and high on the edge of the mesa I seemed almost among them. When morning came I saddled up and checked my supplies. If I'd had more I'd have stayed right there until they tired of hunting me, but at most I'd enough for two days. What I'd best do was get on down to the ranch, say my goodbyes, turn that will over to Janet Le Caudy, and ride on out of what was none of my business anyway.

Skirting the cliffs, I found a way where Indians had walked, and rode north. The view from there took a man's breath. I mean, I'd seen some sights but this was one of the finest. Finding a way through the cedars, I skirted the heads of some canyons an' worked my way over to the east rim of the mesa. There I could look east over the Mancos Valley and in the distance could see Maggie's Rock and the ranch land.

There was a narrow switchback trail came down off the rim there, and I took it. Then I headed east, keeping a sharp lookout for travel, but I saw nobody.

This was wild country. There were cattle running, most of the brands unfamiliar although I saw a few Phillips cows amongst them. The main trail was just north of me but I wasn't about to leave tracks on it, so I came around the end of Menefee Mountain and worked my way, keeping away from trails, into Thompson Park.

This was ranching country and there should have been folks working around, but I saw no one and hoped nobody saw me. At the head of Thompson Park I crossed Cherry Creek an' rode up Deadman Canyon. Now I was in back of the ranch, and I found a horse trail that led up the ridge near Maggie's Rock.

When I left Deadman I had to ride through Spring Gulch, a pretty little canyon, both sides covered with trees. This was a place to take my time and I did so. I rode, rifle in hand, ready for anything. So far I'd used my head but also I'd had luck.

Thing that worried my mind was Pan Beacham. Who was he after? And if he was after me, where *was* he? The rest of them were troublesome men, but Pan . . . he was poison, pure poison.

It was already dark when I rode up the lower end of Spring Gulch. I was dead beat and so were the horses although I'd switched saddles once. It was moonlight, so when I fetched up right below Maggie's Rock, I pulled the riggin' off my stock and picketed them. The grass was good, and I was tired. There'd be no coffee tonight.

Tomorrow I would ride down to the ranch, after scouting for trouble, and I'd say my goodbyes, then cut across to Parrott City to see Janet Le Caudy.

Not that she'd be waiting to see me. She probably had forgotten I so much as existed, but I had to give her that will. It was hers, and half that ranch was hers.

That worried me, too. Why, when Phillips left the ranch to Mrs. Hollyrood, didn't he tell her he only owned half of it? That just didn't make sense.

This was no time to think about that. Tired as I was, my thinkin' just wouldn't make sense. Not that my thinkin' was anything to write home about. When it came to stock, like horses an' cattle, well, I could hold my own. At mining with a single jack an' drill I was a good man. Swinging a single jack or double jack can put power in a man's shoulders, and I guess I had that, but that was about the size of it.

It surely didn't look like rain but in these mountains rain could come up almost anytime, so I stowed my gear an' saddles back under a tree where the branches would give it some shelter from any rain that fell.

There was no worry about rattlers at this altitude, for I'd never seen one above seven thousand feet, or for that matter, not often above sixty-five hundred, and judgin' by the plant life I was around seventy-five hundred or better right here.

There'd been rain earlier. It hadn't fallen where I was but I'd heard distant thunder and had seen lightning over the La Platas. Durin' the last hour I'd been travelin' over wet grass and seein' a good many pools left by the heavy showers. Before comin' up to camp I'd let the horses drink their fill at a couple of those pools.

There was one right down yonder where water had gathered in a slight hollow atop of a boulder. I'd go there and get my own drink.

Lots of shadows. Trees in clumps, trees standin' alone, big rocks here an' there. This was spooky country at night, but then, most wild country is spooky after dark. I stretched, getting the kinks out of my system.

Rifle in hand, I walked down to that rock where the water was. My lids felt thick and heavy. I was sure enough tired, I was—

I bent over to drink and felt a wicked blow in the back and then the roar of a shot, close by. I hit the grass, rolling, stunned and hurt bad. When I started to rise, another bullet struck a tree with an ugly *whap*, and I rolled again, fighting back panic.

Through a fog of shock and fear I heard a voice. He spoke in a conversational tone, easylike, with no hurry in him. "Got you, Mr. Passin'. If you're not dead you can expect me back come daylight. I got no idea of walkin' into a bullet from a man who's dyin'.

"I aimed true and I got you. I seen it hit an' I seen you fall, an' I got you with my second shot. I heard it hit.

"You give me trouble, Mr. Passin', but I figured you for a cagey one. You'd not go ridin' back down to that ranch without lookin' it over.

"Lookin' it over from where? Had to be that ridge, an' comin' at it from the west? Well, all I had to do was set up there close to Maggie's Rock an' wait. Sure enough, there you come. Your hosses was beat so I figured you'd be, too. Had you dead to rights.

"I wonder who you are, Mr. Passin'? You're somebody I should know, but I been fittin' an' comparin' an' tryin' to make you out. No luck so far. But you're good. You left them others half-crazy with wonderin' where you got to. They wasn't lookin' for three horses, like I was, so when they cut your trail they thought they had the wrong man.

"You ain't goin' no place. You jus' lie there an' die. I'll come around in the mornin', just to make sure, an' maybe I'll turn your stock loose so they won't starve when the grass plays out.

"Good night, Mr. Passin', an' goodbye. See you in hell, sometime."

He walked away and I could hear him go. Later I heard his horse, that was while I could still hear. It was a fight to hold still an' stay conscious. I slipped in my mind but I fought it back. If I moved or groaned he would kill me now. He was just hopin' I'd speak so's he could finish the job. He was just baiting me, waiting.

He knew I was somewhere down there in the dark an' I might be playin' possum, so he was behind a rock somewheres just a-waitin' for me to make a fool of myself, but I didn't go to school to eat lunch. Hurt as I was an' ready to pass out, I had sense enough to keep quiet.

Then I crawled. I had to get away, I had to hide. I had to live, I had to—

Everything faded. I'd crawled into mud, and I had to stop the bleeding. I rolled over on my back and pressed the back of my head into the mud.

My eyes closed and I just lay still. If I could not move, I would die. He'd find me there in the morning, and if I was not dead one easy shot would do it. Or he might just pick up a rock and bash in my skull. He'd been known to do that, too.

I had to move, I had to, I would, I—

FOURTEEN

A spattering on my face, and my eyes opened upon darkness. My eyes opened to the rain, then closed. My head throbbed with a dull, heavy beat. When I tried to move, pain shot through me. Waiting, I forced myself to think.

Pan Beacham had shot me. Only my bending to drink had saved me from instant death. Remembering the feeling and realizing how I felt now, I suspected the bullet had skimmed the top of my right buttock, then had cut a furrow in my back above the right shoulder blade and then hit my skull.

As I was alive, the bullet had probably only grazed my head. Deliberately, I forced myself to think, to reason. I was not going to die. Not here, not now. But if I were to survive I needed to move, to be gone from here before Beacham returned. I could not see enough stars to judge the time. The brief shower was over but there might be another. The clouds were over me but in the west beyond Mesa Verde's bulk the sky was clear.

Now I must move, but first a plan. My duffle. My packs. There were things there I would need. Yet suppose he had not gone? Suppose he was sitting back under a tree out of the rain and watching my packs? It would be a logical thing for him to do.

For a moment I mentally braced myself for the effort, then I rolled over. Pain stabbed through me like a sword, making me gasp from sheer agony, yet now I was on my chest, my hands under me. One hand reached out, groping for my rifle. The shine of moisture on the barrel guided my hand. My other hand grasped a tuft of grass and I tugged, slowly, inch by painful inch, groping my way forward.

High ground. I needed to get to high ground. A rough guess

95

suggested it was some two hundred yards through the brush to the top of the ridge. The ranch house was no more than a mile away and probably less. They would help me, and I would need help, but how was I to get there? And crawling as I was would leave a trail any child could follow. Long before I could reach help Pan Beacham or some other enemy would find me.

There was another thought. There were mountain lions ranging the ridge. I had seen their tracks and their droppings. Bears, also, and in the daytime, buzzards.

Slowly, painfully, I crawled. My eyes were accustomed to the dark, and sometimes I could see. There were open spaces among the trees and I crawled through them, dragging the rifle. My head felt heavy and I had to stop. Resting my head on the wet grass, I think I passed out. Maybe I just slept. Then I was crawling again, inching through brush. At a tree with low branches I tugged myself up to my knees, waited for a slow minute, and then managed to get to my feet. Leaning against a tree I felt for my gun. It was still in its holster, the loop over the hammer holding it secure.

What I wanted was to lie down. I wanted to pass out, I wanted just to rest, but to sleep was to die. How much time remained? I did not know. The sky had clouded over and no stars remained. It was going to rain again. Now I could move faster but not much faster. I could reach from tree to tree, from bush to bush, inching my way up the ridge. Several times I fell, and each time it was harder to rise.

There was gray light on the eastern horizon before I topped out on the ridge, and I needed a place to hide. No doubt there were caves or hollows in the sides of Maggie's Rock but I had no time to look nor any wish to dispute their possession with a mountain lion.

Lowering myself carefully to a seat on a flat rock, I got out my bandanna neckerchief and wiped my rifle free of mud and leaves. Then checked the action. It worked.

One thing I knew. If I was to hide, it had to be close. I could go no further. The ranch was almost within sight, and would have been but for the trees, but I hadn't the strength to go on without rest, and the ridge on which I sat offered nothing. To the south it dropped off steeply, in some places sheer for thirty or forty feet, in others just trees and brush through which I'd climbed. On the other side of the ridge it was even steeper and more thickly clad with ponderosa. There was a vague trail along the crest of the ridge and—

Stones, a small square of stones at ground level. Hobbling, I crossed to it, and looked into a hole about five feet deep and roughly two feet square, perhaps a little larger.

I knew what it was. Such holes were used by Indians to trap eagles when they wanted their feathers. An Indian would crouch down in the hole and it would be covered with a lid of woven branches. Atop this he would have a live rabbit tied. Its struggles to escape would attract an eagle, and when it swooped to take the rabbit the Indian would seize its legs.

No sooner had I recognized what it was than I began weaving a lid from pine boughs. Hobbling to the nearest tree, I cut several and wove them into a rough square large enough to cover the hole. Into the crude matt I wove some dead boughs also, and covered it with scattered leaves, then placed it close beside the hole. If need be, that was my refuge. Then I made a dragging track further along the dim trail and to the edge of the cliff on the side where the ranch lay. By the time I got back to my refuge, the sun was in the sky and I was completely exhausted.

From the rim I peered through the trees at the place where I had originally fallen. Some two hundred yards back toward the opening of Spring Gulch was a bay horse, a saddled horse tied to a tree.

Finding its rider required several minutes, and when my eyes discovered him he was squatting in the rocks looking at the place where I had fallen into the mud near a puddle of rainwater. He was a cautious killer, and now he was wondering what had become of me and how far I had managed to get.

My horses and outfit were there, evidence enough that I was out of action. From where he squatted he would be able to see where I had been crawling. Now his eyes were following my route.

For a moment I was tempted to try a shot, but shooting sharply down- or uphill could be tricky. One is apt to over- or undershoot, and my shot must be a kill or he would have me. My position would have been given away, also that I was close by, and he would have all the advantage of being able to maneuver, and I would not. My one chance was the hole. Stepping carefully on rocks, I went to the hole and eased myself into it, gasping with pain. Crouching low, I eased the crude cover in place. Surrounded by small brush, I hoped his eyes would pass quickly over it. And if he came to look, I had my rifle.

Slowly, my tired muscles relaxed. Rifle in hand, I waited. Slowly, I closed my eyes, but not to sleep, merely to rest, for to sleep now might be to snore or even breathe heavily, and that could give me away.

It was a long wait. My back stung and my head throbbed with that same dull, heavy ache. It felt like something pressing on the back of my skull, and when I moved my head it must be with infinite care or I would almost black out. Minutes passed, then ever so softly, and almost above me, a boot brushed the earth. To step on my lid Beacham must step over brush, and it was unlikely for the direction led elsewhere.

Another step, and I could hear him breathing. I dared make no slightest move. My rifle muzzle was within inches of the lid over my hole and my finger was on the trigger.

He would not be looking for or suspecting any such hiding place. No one would. Such holes were uncommon, and always on high places where eagles flew. He might not even know of the trick the Indians used. Not many did. It would be the last thing he would suspect.

He would be looking around rocks, among trees. If he suspected, all he had to do was shoot into the lid, for there would be no escaping. I quite filled the hole. The only way to move was out.

All was quiet. Boots scuffed earth, moving away. My eyes closed again but my ears strained for sound. Thank God he did not have a dog! Boots grated again, and again he was standing close by. He was puzzled.

He knew I was shot. He was sure I was badly hurt. A good marksman knows where his bullets go, and but for the fact that I had bent to drink I would be dead.

I had crawled. He had seen that in the track I left. Later, I had managed to get on my feet but had fallen again and again. He would have seen that, too. So how could I get away? I simply had to be close by. He was obviously disturbed but wary, also. A man who can move is a man who can shoot. He might not suspect me of having a rifle unless he checked both saddles, for the other rifle was in its scabbard and he might have seen that. It would be unlikely he would suspect me of having two rifles, which was the case due to the outfit inherited with the blue roan.

He struck a match on his jeans. I heard the scrape and the flare. He was lighting a cigarette. He flipped the burned-out match and it fell on the lid above me. From time to time his boots moved.

My legs were cramped and the strain was becoming unbearable. He walked off a few steps, then came back.

An awful thought came. He knew I was there! He was amusing himself, deliberately torturing me. Supposing he decided to build a fire atop my hole? That was ridiculous because it was among small but highly inflammable brush. If only I could straighten out, stretch my cramped legs!

My thoughts concentrated on his horse. If I thought of him he might somehow sense my thoughts. I did not believe that but had heard of such things, so to keep my thoughts from him I thought of his horse. Somebody was going to steal his horse. Somebody was going to set him afoot. Somebody—

He moved away but not far away. Finally he swore softly, bitterly, then his footsteps retreated off down the trail. I waited. I counted a slow one hundred, and there was no sound. Again I counted, slower still, something to measure the passing of time. Still I waited.

How long had I been in this hole? An hour? Two hours? I could not get at my watch to see. Again I waited. He might be lying close by, hoping I would appear from whatever hiding place I'd chosen.

My lids were heavy, and I was tired. All I wanted was to get out of this hole and sleep. If I could only get down to the ranch!

Somehow, some way, I fell asleep, and when I awakened it was a long time later. It was time to get out of this hole, to get away from here. I needed care for my wound, I needed water, I needed food, and I needed decent rest. I started to move, then stopped.

A movement, right close by. Only the slightest move in the brush. A hacking sound, then a voice, low, conversational. That was Pan Beacham, all right. Talking to himself.

"Lucky I brought this Bowie. Handy to have." More hacking and then something dropped over the hole where I crouched. One of the interstices between branches of my lid was suddenly blocked out. Somebody had dropped a pile of brush right over my head!

"A fire," his voice said, "that's what I need. A fire. Throw some light on the subject. Nothin' better than a good fire to bring things out into the open."

Fire! He was building a fire! Somehow, some way he had figured it out! He knew where I was hiding. My muscles gathered for a lunge, then slowly relaxed. The fire would burn up, and only ashes might drop on me. Still—

A thought came, bringing a sharp arrow of hope. He had to light the fire. If he lit a piece of brush and threw it on the pile, I was done for, but suppose he struck a match and leaned close to touch it to the fuel?

Most men would do that. I listened for the sound of his boots, heard them crush leaves close by. He was squatting. I could hear his breathing. He struck a match and I glimpsed some of its flame. There was a shadow as he leaned over to light the fire. I shoved the rifle up hard and as it touched his body I pulled the trigger.

The concussion in that small hole was shocking. I lunged desperately to get out of the hole, away from the fire. I lunged and fell across Beacham, who was trying to rise. He pushed me away, reaching for the Bowie. My hand shot out, grasping at the knife, and our hands gripped.

Frantic to escape the growing fire, I swung a fist against his chin. The effort sent a stab of pain through me, but I struggled to rise. He had the Bowie, but as I reached one knee I drove the muzzle of the rifle up under his chin and he staggered back. There was blood all over him and his eyes were wild.

He fell backward and I lost balance and fell, too. Grabbing a handful of flaming brush, I thrust it into his face, but he knocked it away and scrambled to his feet.

"Damn you! You got me! Damn—!" He was clawing for a pistol.

Kicking out, my boot caught him on the knee and he fell into the scattered fire. Rolling over, I got the loop off my pistol and drew. As he came up again I put three bullets into him.

He swore again, slowly, viciously. I pulled my leg away from the fire, resting on my left elbow, the gun in my right hand.

"Damn you all to hell!" he said, and died.

FIFTEEN

For a moment I just stayed where I was and then I got up. My wounds were bleeding. I could feel blood running down my leg. Standing wide-legged, braced against another fall, I emptied the three spent shells from my pistol and reloaded. Then I holstered the gun and slipped the thong back in place.

The fire he had tried to light had been scattered and was burning down in the hole and also in a few scattered leaves. One by one I put them out, looking around for any I might have missed.

Then I recovered my rifle. My brain was foggy and my eyes seemed hard to focus. When I looked at something it needed a moment for what I saw to register.

Through it all there was a struggling thread of sanity. I was hurt, badly hurt, and I needed care, rest and care. To get back down to my horses would be a struggle, but then I must ride for some distance around to get to the ranch. It would be better to keep going along the ridge and find a trail right to the ranch. Once there, Matty and Mrs. Hollyrood would care for me.

Vaguely there was the thought that our shooting might have attracted attention, but I did not know how far the sound would carry nor if anyone was within hearing distance. Going straight down the cliff was out of the question. It was too steep in the first place and I'd walked through tangles like that before and knew I'd never make it.

Further along, as I remembered from having studied the ridge, there was more open country. There were brush and trees but not the tangle there was close by. Weak though I was, I simply had to try. If I could only get to the ranch!

Carrying my rifle, I walked steadily east along the ridge, catching an occasional glimpse of the ranch through the trees. Mostly I stared straight ahead, trying to walk straight, trying to keep going. Once, when a flat rock was beside the dim trail, I sat down.

My wounds seemed to have stopped bleeding but my shirt was stuck to my back with blood and my hair was matted with it. Somehow I'd kept my hat.

Now I could see the ranch buildings, the big barn, the corrals, and the granary. At the corral across from the house there was a rig and a team of horses. At the distance I could make out no details except I could see the sun on the buggy. It looked to be all slick and varnished like that outfit I'd seen in Parrott City.

A trail slanted down the ridge through the ponderosa and I started down but hadn't gone far when I had to stop. I sat down on a fallen log, feeling all weak and faint. I'd lost blood, and now the excitement of my fight for life was wearing off. I was weak as a rabbit.

There was shade under the pines and I sat down and kind of leaned back against the trunk of a tree. My eyes closed and I guess I just fell asleep. How long I was there I don't know, maybe only a few minutes, maybe an hour. When I opened my eyes again I was all stiff and sore and it was hard to move. For a moment I just sat there looking across at all the magnificence of the La Platas rearing up beyond the ranch. I could see smoke rising from a chimney in Parrott City, and from a mine further east. I just sat there, too weak to rise, but feeling the urge to move on. Down below and not far from the foot of the ridge I could see water in a pool. Not far from it, cattle grazed. Then coming in from the east, and keeping down behind the trees and riding where there was low ground, I saw three horsemen.

For several minutes I watched them without it making any impression. They were just part of the scenery along with the mountains, the trees, and the brush, then slowly realization began to get through to me.

One of those riders, judging by the horse he rode, must be Lew Paine!

My thoughts came into focus and I sat up, staring at them. They were riding through the trees, keeping out of sight of the ranch. Now they drew up and one of them was standing in his stirrups, looking toward the ranch. They were a good half-mile away but I was several hundred feet higher and could see them clearly. Now they were apparently talking.

Maybe whatever they planned did not include the presence of that buggy.

Several meadows started narrow between folds of the hills but widened out as they drew nearer the ranch house. The trail I was on apparently ended in or skirted one of those meadows. The riders, if they kept on as going, would emerge in another meadow just over a knoll from the one I was headed for.

The last thing I wanted right now was trouble. I'd had my fill. I was hurt and mighty weak from the blood I'd lost, needing water and something to eat, but mostly just rest and to get my wounds cleaned and treated.

Who set Pan Beacham on me I had no idea, but for a man who wanted no trouble I was having aplenty. Now if those riders down below found me they'd make short work of me. I was in no shape for a stand-up fight of any kind. One thing about my wounds. In this high-up country the early mountain men had begun to notice that wounds healed more rapidly than in the lowlands where there were lots of people. Probably there was less corruption in the air. That thought was small comfort.

Those men down below seemed to be studying what they'd do. Maybe that buggy posed a problem. Likely they were figuring they'd find nobody to home but those womenfolks. They'd been scouting around and they might know I'd ridden away over west and they might even know about Beacham hunting me. So they'd be sure they had a clear field for whatever they had in mind. Now that buggy was creating a problem.

What would they do? Most likely they'd find someplace from which to watch and just wait. So if I was careful and could keep from sight until right at the ranch house I'd be able to make it.

Well, I got up. It was something of a struggle but I had the rifle to help me and I made my feet and turned down trail. Stiff an' sore as I was, I couldn't move fast. I was lucky to even be moving. The sky was still overcast, and there was a hint of rain. Slowly, I started down the path, keeping under cover of the trees so if anybody looked my way I'd not be seen.

My shirt was stuck to my back with dried blood but I daren't work it loose because it might start bleeding again. That time I got no more than thirty or forty steps before I just had to stop. There was no place to sit but the ground and I knew I'd never be able to get up again, so I just leaned against the bank on the high side of the trail.

Through the trees I could make out that buggy. It looked like the same outfit I'd seen driven into Parrott City as I was leaving, the one driven by the fellow whom I had suspected of being Janet's friend. But what would he be doing out here? Unless he had driven her out for a conference.

The riders down below were now out of my sight. My trail switched and angled away from them. After a rest, I heaved myself erect, tottered a little, then went on, a step at a time. Once or twice I nearly faded out, and I had a hunch I just wasn't going to make it. Not this time, anyway.

If those riders found me in this shape I'd be easy pickings. I doubted I had strength more than to lift my rifle. God forbid they should ride up this trail.

Somebody had worked on this trail in times past. It was wide enough for one rider or walker, and part of it was cut into the mountainside, leaving a steep bank on one side, a thick stand of ponderosa on the other. Occasionally there were thin spots where I could see through to the ranch buildings. There seemed to be no activity outside.

My knees were weak and I felt woozy. I walked on, seeing a fallen tree ahead of me. When I got there I rewarded myself with the promise that I'd sit down. Twice I simply stopped, gathering my strength to go on, and when I made it I sank to a seat with a gasp. Dizzy, I had a hard time making my eyes focus. My face felt hot and my mouth dry. Desperately, I wished for a drink but there was no water. If I could just make the house I'd be safe.

Head hanging, I sat on the dead tree only dimly aware of time or place. My eyes closed and the moments drifted slowly by. A cool wind came off the La Platas where now clouds gathered, and I hunched my shoulders, only barely conscious. Vaguely an old tune from a music hall ran through my mind, and I chuckled at some forgotten memory. When at last I tried to rise I fell, to my knees first, then to my face on the trail, my face among the fallen leaves.

A long time later a cool wind blew and I shivered, and opened my eyes. For a time I simply lay there, content to be lying, content to be resting. After a little while I rolled to my face and got my knees under me and sat up. I must move. I must get off this trail. I must—

Using the rifle as a crutch again I struggled to my feet and tottered down the trail. It had been hours since I'd been shot, hours since I'd started down the trail.

Where were the riders? Holed up, watching for her visitor to go so they might attack the place?

My back was stiff and I moved carefully so as not to begin bleeding again. When I had made a hundred steps, I found a place to sit down and rest, listening for the riders who must be within two hundred yards of me and probably much less. Looking ahead, I could see the trail I was on sort of disappeared in rank undergrowth. The area had been cut over at some time and brush had grown up, yet there was a sort of trail left by deer. After a few minutes I struggled to my feet and started on. Soon I was in thick brush and scrub oak where I could see no more than a few feet. Nor could I see the house or other buildings as they were now hidden from view.

Emerging from the brush on the upper end of a meadow, I kept close to the wall of brush and scrub oak that covered the low hill that lay between me and the riders. If I guessed correctly they were either hidden somewhere opposite me, and probably not over a hundred yards away, or they might be skirting the same low hill in the meadow east of it.

Twice I stumbled and fell. Each time it was harder to rise. Yet in the moments when I could think clearly I did not believe I was seriously wounded. There had been shock, of course, and I'd lost blood, a lot of blood. The one bullet seemed to have caused three wounds, hitting me as it did when I was lying down.

Soon it would be night. If only I could reach the house! Reach it without coming under the guns of Lew Paine and his companions.

When I next came in sight of the buildings I was behind a thin screen of low trees on a bluff looking right down into the ranch yard.

All was quiet. The buckskin I had ridden was in the corral, not fifty yards away. The spanking-new buggy was still there, the team tied to the corral railing.

What was going on down there? Uneasily, I studied the layout. That buggy had been here for hours, and if that was Janet Le Caudy's friend he was spending a lot of time with

Mrs. Hollyrood and Matty. Perhaps he had known them before? Or it might be somebody else?

I lay quiet. The ranch buildings might be within view of Lew Paine and his men, certainly they were close by, and I did not want to give away my presence or the fact that I was hurt.

In an hour or less it would be dark. Pillowing my head on my arm, I rested, waiting.

Somehow, I fell asleep, and when I awakened the buggy was gone and night had fallen. Very carefully, I sat up, feeling a stab of pain from my back. My body was stiff and the night had chilled me.

Awareness came slowly. I was badly hurt. I was in trouble. My enemies might be close by.

There were lights in the house. A shadow passed the window curtain. Using the rifle to help, I got to my feet. Listening, I heard no slightest sound, and with care I started around to come down off the bluff. To do that I must go either east or west, but to the east was where Lew Paine had been so I chose west. Carefully, trying to make no sound, taking only a step at a time, I went westward, came down off the slope, and keeping close to the low bluff so as to throw no shadow, I started toward the small bridge that crossed the creek.

The granary was dark. For a few minutes I waited beside some willows, then crossed to the granary. Again I paused to listen. My head ached with a slow, heavy throbbing that made it hard to concentrate. All I could think of was that bed and washing some of the blood from my body and getting a cold drink of water. I needed help, and I needed some care. Maybe I could get it here.

Somewhere I heard movement, but listening intently, I heard nothing more. Crossing the road, I lifted the latch and stepped inside, closing the door after me. Then pausing, I listened for any sound that might imply somebody was there. Hearing nothing, I stepped to the bed. It was as I had left it. Remembering Lew Paine, I struck no light, but went back to the door and drew the latch string inside so the door could not be opened from the outside.

Slowly my eyes became accustomed to the inner darkness. Before leaving, knowing I'd be gone for a while, I'd brought the washbasin inside, and there was a bucket of water. First off, I drank, then drank again. Then I washed my face and using a piece of an old towel I soaked some of the dried blood out of my hair.

When I'd cleaned up a mite I just couldn't make it any further. I stretched out on the bed and slept, my pistol beside me, my rifle within reach. Before I stretched out I held my watch to the window and could just make out the time. It was only just past nine o'clock.

A low rapping awakened me. A moment there I thought I was dreaming, then a whisper. Swinging my feet to the floor, I tiptoed over. Again there was that subdued rapping. "Who's there?"

My gun was in my hand and I stood to one side of the door.

"It's me! Matty! Let me in!" The words were whispered, scarcely loud enough for me to hear.

Gun still in hand, I opened the door. She glided in like a ghost. "I saw you come. I've been watching for you! Where is your horse?"

"Up on the mountain. Man tried to kill me."

"I know! Mr. Passin', you've got to leave! You've got to get away! Don't ask me why, just go!"

"Ma'am, I'm bad hurt. Well, maybe not so bad, but I lost blood. I need rest, ma'am, need it bad. I'm all in."

"You must go! They will kill you! Don't ask questions! Just go!"

"Told you, ma'am. I need rest. I couldn't make it to no-wheres. Besides, Lew Paine an' them, they're outside. I mean they're close by! I figure they'll pull somethin' off. I mean they'll attack the place before daybreak. You got to be ready."

"Please! You've got to go!"

"I better see the missus first. I got to warn her."

"Please, Passin', please go! Don't try to see her! Don't even think of her!"

"Well, it ain't hardly polite, you know. She promised to fix me a dinner. I was sort of lookin' forward to it, hungry as I am."

"Don't even think of it. Not unless you want that dinner to be your last. Just get out of here before they know you're here!"

" 'They'?"

"Don't ask questions! Go! I must get back before they know I'm gone or they will kill me, too!"

"Kill *you*? Who?"

She was almost in tears. *"Please!* Just go! Out there you have a chance. Here you've none at all! Please go, *quickly!"*

"Matty?" It was a call from the steps of the house. It was Mrs. Hollyrood.

"Oh, my God!" It was almost a prayer. "Please go! They think you found something, some papers or something in that drawer. And *please!* If they find you and invite you in, don't eat or drink *anything!"*

With that, she was gone, and a moment later I heard her saying, "It was too warm inside. I had to get out in the air." The door closed behind them and I got up and smoothed out the bed, drawing the blanket tight again the way McCarron or whatever his name was had left it.

A moment I waited, rifle in hand. Desperately I wanted to lie down, simply to *sleep.* I'd lost blood, was weak as a cat, and my back was stiff. I wanted—

Easing out of the door, I stood still, black against the blackness of the building. If Lew Paine found me now, this case would be settled by lever action rather than legal action. I was in no shape to argue.

What did Matty mean when she said they thought I had found something in that drawer? How could they know? Then suddenly I felt a chill. Used to noticing things, there was one thing I'd noticed that I'd forgotten about. Those papers had been lying there quite a while and when I picked up the will it had left a brown stain on the papers beneath it, a straight line of brown across the paper underneath, some chemicals in the paper, no doubt. Many a time I'd found a paper in an old book that had discolored the page of the book against which it was pressed. I'd found the tally book but what else?

Stiff as I was, it was not easy but I eased myself betwixt the corral bars and walked over to the buckskin. It shied a little, then stood still. For a moment I stood beside it, speaking softly, then, with a grip on its mane I led it back to the old barn.

Inside it was black as sin, but listening I heard no sound. Walking the horse to a stall where I knew some buckskin strings were hanging as well as a hackamore, I felt for the hackamore, found it, and slipped it over the ears of the buckskin. Took a few of the buckskin piggin' strings.

Walking the horse to the barn door I waited, listening again. *Where was Lew Paine?*

With the reins in my left hand I was fixin' to swing astride when something thrust hard into the small of my back, an' nobody needed to explain to me what it was. Then a low, triumphant voice said, "Lew? Come on! I *got* him!"

SIXTEEN

My arms were up, one hand resting on the buckskin's mane, the right hand reaching for its back, and I knew they intended to kill me.

My right arm came around, the elbow smashing into the man's temple, knocking him away from me. My elbow hit hard, momentarily stunning him. In an instant I was astride, and bending low I caught up my rifle from the end of the stall where it had been leaning and I went out of the barn on a dead run.

The corral gate was before me but they had left it open when they entered, and I went through and swung hard to my left, putting the wall of the barn between us. We thundered across the small bridge and then went up the trail to the meadow on a dead run.

From behind me there was a shot, and turning in the saddle as the buckskin came to a stand, I levered three fast shots at the flash of the gun, and then we were off and running. Over a low hill, then along a trail into the scrub oak.

Once under cover I slowed up, gasping with pain. The sudden, violent movements had ripped open the wounds that had begun to heal. Now they were bleeding again.

Looking back I could see nothing but blackness. The lights in the house had been hastily blown out, and no doubt they were watching, waiting, wondering what was going on.

Sagging in the saddle, completely done in by the sudden burst of action, I rode through the oaks toward Maggie's Rock. How I stayed on that horse, I don't know. When a man has been riding all his life he can fall asleep in the saddle or be half-conscious and his instinct or something will still keep him riding.

The rifle was my worry, so taking a couple of the rawhide strings I'd fetched along I rigged a sling for it and slung it across my back.

The clouds had gone and the stars were out. For a man who'd been out all night, seeing was easy. It was coming up to daylight when I rounded the base of Maggie's Rock and rode up Spring Gulch to where I'd left my outfit.

Everything was there, so I saddled up, and leading my spare horses I went up the trail to the little valley atop the ridge and below Maggie. Looking up from the ranch nobody would ever guess there was a valley up here, and I dearly needed rest.

With the last strength I had left I staked out my horses and rolling over on the grass I pulled a saddle blanket across my shoulders.

At some time during the morning it rained, a brief shower only. Vaguely I was aware of it but slept on, oblivious to all by my complete exhaustion. When finally my eyes did open it was midafternoon. By then the sun had dried the grass. For a time I lay still, watching the lazy circles of a buzzard in the sky. At last I sat up, taking in my surroundings with gathering comprehension.

Directly west was Maggie's Rock. The trail, dim and unused, led past where I lay, along the bottom of the small valley and into the trees beyond Maggie. The north side of the valley was a low ridge, wooded to the top, and a trail led along it and back up to the higher ridge where I had killed Pan Beacham.

The place where I lay was under a big ponderosa and there were numerous pinecones lying about. Clearing away the pine needles and grass with my hands, I broke twigs from low on the tree and put together a small fire. The twigs, long-dead suckers, were perfectly dry. Gathering some other fallen sticks, I made a small fire, allowing the smoke to rise through the tree and thin itself before going into the air.

From my pack I got my coffeepot, frying pan, and then coffee and bacon. Taking my time as I tired rapidly, I made coffee and fried a dozen strips of bacon.

My little camp was in a niche under the trees and would be invisible to anyone until they were close upon me. When I had eaten the bacon I sat back with a cup of coffee in my hand, leaning against the trunk of a ponderosa, and studied my situation.

All I wanted was to get out of here, to get away from everybody. I wanted to be back in the mountains where I belonged. Here I was, just passin' through the country, and suddenly the roof fell in. First that Houston Burrows tried to kill me, then that roan horse brought me to the ranch and into all kinds of trouble. Well, I had my gear and I was going to ride on and keep riding.

Why had Matty been in such an all-fired hurry to get shut of me? She didn't even want Mrs. Hollyrood to know I was around. Apparently getting rid of me was more important than anything the Paine outfit might do. And what did she mean by saying Mrs. Hollyrood had found where I'd taken some papers from that drawer? She'd told me to look there for the book, told me herself.

Something was wrong and I was beginning to wonder if I didn't already have the answer.

When I had rested I would pack my horse, saddle the others, and ride for Parrott City. There were a few things I needed before moving into wild country. Yet even as I told myself that, I knew what I really wanted was to see Janet Le Caudy and give her the will I had. Once I'd done that I'd have no further part in what took place, yet even as I told myself that, I knew, uneasily, that what I really wanted to do was see Janet Le Caudy again. Not that she meant anything to me or ever could.

Now I was thirsty. Luckily the canteen was still half-full and I drank from it. The water wasn't too good, it had been in the canteen for several days, but then I'd drunk worse, much worse. The fever I had as well as the loss of blood might have much to do with my thirst.

Before I packed, I'd rest some more. I moved the picket pins of my horses to give them fresh grazing and then returned to the shade of the ponderosas.

The cattle I'd seen running on the ranch worried me. There should be a roundup and a culling of the herd. Steers would do better on winter range than cows, and somebody should be out there now, rounding up some of the cows and bringing them in to feed before shipping. With the railroad right close, shipping would be easy, to either Kansas City or Denver. Some of this stock was pretty wild but I'd always favored wilder cattle, they lived longer and fattened up quicker on poor range. They were tough, and cattle were like men or mustangs, it took the tough ones to survive when times were bad. Men could become tough but cattle that had been living well seemed to give up easier.

Through the afternoon I dozed and dreamed and thought, and before sundown I brought in my horses, and taking it easy, I saddled up, packed up, and hit the trail. By the time I got into the saddle I was worn out. I mean, I was tired. Not to follow the same route, I went back down into Spring Gulch and rode east along the grassy bottom. Up at the far end I found a water hole and watered my horses.

There was a horse trail to the top of the ridge and I took it, walking my horses and stopping now and again to give them a time to catch air. By the time I topped out on the ridge above that beautiful grove of aspen through which I'd ridden a few days before, it was last light.

Up yonder, liking the cool breeze, I sat my saddle looking back toward the ranch. There was a slow lift of blue smoke from the ranch-house chimney but no other sign of life. Right then I turned that buckskin loose.

He knew where his home was and chances were he'd go back. A horse just naturally doesn't like to leave home but he doesn't like to leave other horses, either. If he followed me into town I wasn't to blame for that. I'd have no rope on him and they couldn't accuse me of stealin' him. But chances are he would go back to where he'd been fed.

The way I chose led down into the aspen again. Already the leaves were beginning to change color, fall was coming on, and they'd soon turn all to gold and that trail I was riding would be like walking down an aisle through a great golden cathedral. The leaves whispered, moving gently on the stems.

Before I rode into the main trail I drew up to give it study. Nobody in sight. Nothing moving, anywhere. Somewhere afar off I heard a train whistle.

Then I rode down from the trees, trotted my horse across the trail and into the woods. Less than an hour later, and in full darkness, I rode into Parrott.

There were a dozen lighted buildings along the street. I took my horses to a corral that did duty as a livery stable and stripped the gear from them. There was a small shed close by where a man in a beat-up hat told me I could leave my saddles and gear. "Safe," he said, "nobody steals nothin' around here."

The half-dollar I gave him loosened his tongue. "Seen you around," he commented, "talkin' with that Le Caudy gal."

"Nice girl," I said, casually.

"Yep. Seems so." He lit his pipe, threw the match into the dust, and spat. "She's takin' up with the wrong folks. Feller with a blond mustache, looks like a city feller."

"Seen him around. You know him?"

"His kind. He's a gambler or some woman's fancy man. But don't you take him light. That's an uncommon bad man." He glanced at me from the corners of his eyes. "Carries a sleeve gun. One o' them derringers, y'know. In a holster up his sleeve. Lifts his hand and it slides out, drops his hand down an' it slides right into his hand an' nobody sees it. Mostly they'd be watchin' the gun in the holster on his hip. Seen him give it a try in the shed there when he figured nobody was lookin'."

"Now that's right neighborly. Do the same for you, sometime."

"That there Le Caudy girl, she's a decent woman. Anybody can see it, yet he's got around her somehow, offered to help."

"I was wonderin' why." Pausing, I said, "Between the two of us, she's owner of half that ranch down on Cherry Creek. I figure she really owns it all."

"Where the women are?"

"That one. I been fixin' up around. The place needs work."

"I know it. Phillips, he let it run down there toward the end. He was off chasin' after some woman."

"Mrs. Hollyrood."

"That her name? Figured it was the young one." He paused. "That young one? I seen her somewheres before."

"Where?"

He shrugged. "Don't recall." He drew on his pipe, then swore. It had gone out. "Lived over in Denver for a while. I was jailer there." He looked at me. "Maybe I ain't seen her. Maybe I seem a flyer on her. Y'know? Them 'wanted' bills that come in? You held the job. I can tell by the way you move into a town. You've worn a badge."

"Janet Le Caudy? She in town?"

"She is right now but she won't be in the mornin'. I heard that Pelham feller offer to drive her down to the ranch on Cherry Creek. He said he'd drive her down tomorrow. Said he'd make inquiries on how to get there."

"He drive that smart new buggy?"

"Yep."

"He was down there today, most of the day."

Walking up the street, I got myself a bed in a three-bed room, then went across the dusty lane to get myself a bait of grub. I was hopin' she'd be in there and she was. She was settin' up to the table an' she was alone.

"Oh? I thought you were gone."

"I came back."

She looked at me very thoughtfully. "You look as if you had been ill? I mean, you're very pale."

"I had some trouble." I put my cup down. "Ma'am? If I was you, I'd get a good lawyer. I'd go into Animas City or this new town they've started and I'd get a lawyer. You're goin' to need one."

"I have a friend who is helping me."

"Pelham? Is that right? Known him long?"

"No, but—"

"Tell you where he was today?"

"No, why should he? As a matter of fact, I haven't seen him today."

"I haven't either, but that rig he drives was out at the Phillips ranch most of the day."

"But that couldn't be. Today he was to drive over to Mancos on business. He told me so."

"The rig was there most of the day."

She smiled. "You must be mistaken. There are many buggies that are similar." She looked at me coolly over her cup. "If you knew about that rig you must have been there yourself."

"Yes, ma'am. I was laid up. I mean, I'd been shot. Right about then I was just tryin' to stay alive."

"*Shot?*" She was shocked.

"Yes, ma'am. Somebody follered me. Taken a shot at me only he didn't kill me like he intended. I moved and the bullet sort of cut me in the back and bounced off my skull." I turned my head a little to show her. "I put some pine sap on the wound to stop the bleeding. It works pretty good."

"You haven't seen a doctor?"

"No, ma'am. It's like the law out here. They are never around when you need them."

"But *why*? Why would someone try to shoot you like that?"

I shrugged. "Has to do somethin' with that ranch. Of course, there's the Burrows outfit. They want me dead but they haven't the money to hire the man who was after me. I know him and he comes high. Either somebody is ready to pay a lot of money to have me killed or he owes somebody a favor. Anyway, he tried."

A rider went by in the street, then it was quiet again. Dishes rattled in the kitchen. It was late and probably we were the last customers they'd have. Western towns were early-to-sleep towns except for the saloons and gambling houses.

"Won't he try again?"

"No, ma'am."

"You mean he's—*dead*?"

"In his business, in this country, a man like that makes a mistake just once."

It was quiet in the room again and we ate without speaking. "I am afraid," she said after a bit, "it is more violent out here than I believed."

"No, ma'am. Mostly this is a quiet kind of country. Good folks here, and hardworking. The people making trouble are outsiders."

"Aren't you an outsider?"

"Yes, ma'am, an' one who's fixin' to leave as soon as this ranch business gets straightened out."

"Why should that concern you?"

That was a good question. It was none of my business, except that in my pocket I had a will, and with the kind of friend she had I wasn't about to give it to her. Not yet, anyway.

We had finished eating but there was something more I wished to say. She stood up. "Thank you for your advice, Mr. Passin'." Her eyes were cool. "I do not believe we will be seeing each other again."

"I am here if you need me."

She gave me that cool, straight look again. "I shall not need you."

"You may, when they find out you own half their ranch."

"What do you mean?"

"That will she's got leaves it all to her. Like you never existed, an', ma'am? You be careful."

"I am always careful, Mr. Passin'. Now—good evening."

She turned away but I stood my ground. "If you go out there, an' they invite you to eat, or even drink something, take my advice and don't."

"What does that mean?"

"I don't rightly know, only your uncle, Phillips, he had supper with them."

She walked outside and crossed the street to the hotel. I waited a minute, studying the street. Behind me somebody was gathering dishes from our vacated table. "Mister? We're closin' up now—"

"I know. Would you mind blowing out that lamp?"

When the room was dark I waited close to the door, then opened it very gently and stepped out into the dark.

SEVENTEEN

The blacksmith, a big Dutchman, had rigged some barrels out back of his place for bathing at two bits the bath. With a towel and some fresh clothing from my pack I went around to the barrels. Nobody was anywhere around, and after waiting a bit to be sure nobody was around, I took a long bath, dried off, and dressed in fresh clothes, keeping my six-shooter at hand.

The hotel room I had, if you could call it that, was shared by two other men, both of them already asleep. I went to the cot where I'd piled my gear earlier and turned in, and was up at daybreak dressing. One of the men was already gone, and the other noticed the long, red, barely healed streak along my back.

"None o' my business," he commented, "but looks like you lucked out."

"It was close."

"Healin' all right?"

"In this mountain air they heal up fast."

He was anxious to know more but too polite to ask questions and I wasn't planning to answer any. By the time I was dressed, having to take time with my shirt, and he did give me a hand there, it was already light outside.

Going past Janet's room, I slipped a note under the door:
Make them come to you.

Then I went down to breakfast, and the place was almost full of folks, most of them men. They were eating quick breakfasts and some were picking up lunch pails they'd left to be filled for the day.

There was a place empty at the end of the table near the kitchen and I sat there. Most of the men eating had guns in

118

sight except for several who had on their diggin' clothes and were headed for a mine somewhere. There were several mines about employing men and a couple of dozen prospect holes men were working on their own.

Taking my time, I let the crowd thin out. The cook came over to fill my cup again and stood, dryin' his hands on his apron. "You stickin' around?"

My eyes reached him from under my brows. "Passin' through," I said, "sometimes it takes a while."

"I hear talk. I hear Paine and his boys been huntin' you."

"They found me a couple of times. If they're smart they'll ride off into the hills and round up some strays."

"Nobody ever said they were smart."

"A couple more days an' I'll drift."

He sat down across from me and filled a cup. "That Pinkerton feller? He was talkin' to me, figured me friendly to you."

"I hope you are."

"He said you should fight shy of those women, yonder."

I drank my coffee.

"He said you had troubles enough without them. He said I should tell you that Pan Beacham wasn't the right name, that Pan had him a brother somewheres about."

"All right. I had an idea it was something like that." I looked over at him. "You tell him that if Pan was on his list he can scratch the name."

He looked at me again, shaking his head. "You're a hard man, Passin', a hard man."

Well, I let that pass. Maybe I was, an' maybe I wasn't, only I like to be let alone and I've a bad feelin' about folks shooting at me. I don't take to it. Never did.

"A brother, you say?"

"That's right. Pan was a man who had a strong family feelin', they say. He an' his brother, do anything for one another."

"It's a good way to be." I paused, looking into my cup. "I never had a brother. No sister, either, come to that, nor much of any kinfolk." I looked over at him. "Never had anything but a few good horses."

"You still ridin' that blue roan?"

"That's a horse. That's the best of them. Him an' me, we both got bad names without huntin' for 'em. I never wanted anything but the quiet of the high-up hills." I looked at him again. "Never had anything, either. Not a pot nor a window to throw it out of."

"You never had you a woman?"

"Not one to keep." I moved irritably. "Womenfolks don't see much in me. Sometimes they look twice, then they look for somebody else. I'm a hard man, and I guess it shows."

He went back to his kitchen and I set by with what was left of my meal. This feller was a good cook and that trail crew he rode with must have been contented men. Me, I just sat there havin' no place to go and nobody wantin' me anywhere. I set there thinkin' of how a man can't always stay in the high-up hills and when the snows fall he's got to get out of the mountains before he gets snowed in. Life was about to get me snowed in. Suddenly I was tired of sleeping in a room with a bunch of other men, having no more home than the cot I slept in.

About that time Janet Le Caudy came in and with her was that Charles Pelham Clinton. They sat down well away from me although he shot me a quick, hard look, and I remembered he wore a sleeve gun up his right sleeve.

Janet kept her eyes well away from me, but in that small area there was no way I couldn't hear them talk.

"No reason why we can't settle it today." He took out a gold watch from his vest pocket and looked at it. "As a matter of fact, I will have to be leaving soon, so if I am to help you it must be today."

"All right."

"I am sure Mrs. Hollyrood is a reasonable woman. If you are half-owner as you say, I am sure she will recognize your rights. In any event, I believe she wishes to leave. The ranch isn't quite what she expected from hearing Mr. Phillips speak of it. She had a somewhat exaggerated idea of what it might be like. I believe you could buy her out or reach some agreement."

The cook came out looking wise and refilled my cup. He also brought me a slab of pie.

"You might as well bring your things. From all I hear there will be room enough at the ranch, and there's no use to stay on here. I know," he added, "the conditions here are hardly suitable for a lady."

"I am all right. It is a nice clean room." Her voice was subdued.

"You have, I suppose"—he paused a little and tried to speak

lower—"papers here to support your claim? She will be wanting to see anything you have."

"Of course." She hesitated, and made a move as if to glance my way, but did not.

Like she had said, it was none of my business, and by mixing into it, all I'd managed was to get shot at. For a peaceful man who only wants to live in the high-up hills I was findin' all sorts of trouble. Nevertheless, I didn't like it.

She should get herself a lawyer and she shouldn't trust strangers, including me. But I wasn't tryin' to get her out to a ranch where she'd be far from anywhere.

There was some kind of a tie-up between Clinton and Mrs. Hollyrood or Matty, but I didn't know what. They were new to this country, although Clinton acted like he'd been around.

A young woman like that, there were plenty of folks around whom she could appeal to who would be glad to help, just good honest folk who would advise her and stand by.

Clinton glanced around at me, and I knew my being there was bothering him, irritating him, I should say. My eyes were on my coffee cup, apparently paying them no mind. He pushed back and got up.

"In about thirty minutes, then? You will be ready? Bring all your things."

"All right."

Was I mistaken or did she sound a mite reluctant? If she was having second thoughts she'd best have them quick.

He stood as if expecting her to rise, but she didn't. She looked up at him and said, "I'm going to have another cup of coffee, Mr. Clinton."

"Call me Pell." He hesitated, obviously wanting her out of here, but there was nothing more he could say. "All right. I'll get the team."

When he had gone, nobody spoke for a few minutes, just sitting there drinking our coffee. I wanted no more of it, but it was an excuse to stay on. She glanced my way a couple of times, then she said, almost defiantly, "I'm going out to the ranch."

"I heard."

"I just must get this settled at once. I can't afford to stay on here like this."

"Why does he want you to bring your gear? To a business meeting?"

"He knows I can't afford to stay on here so he thought I should stay at the ranch."

"With a couple of people you don't know? Who won't be too happy to find they don't own the whole ranch? Ma'am, like you said, this is none of my affair. I'm buttin' in where I'm not wanted, an' you already read me off. I just wonder why they want you out there when it could all be settled here, in front of witnesses?"

"It wasn't their idea. Mr. Clinton suggested it."

"After spending all yesterday afternoon with them? Ma'am, I think—"

"You don't *know* that! You weren't there! Anyway, what difference could it make to you? You've no right to say those things! He's been very helpful!"

Other folks came in and our talk stopped there. After a minute she put down a quarter to pay for her meal and walked out without so much as a glance my way.

I swore, and a couple of the men who had just come in glanced my way. Then I got up and walked outside. Crossing to the corral, I saddled the roan and tied him there. I'd scarcely finished when Clinton came down the street.

The roan was standing there so I began fussing with the saddle, apparently paying him no mind. He brought out the team, harnessed them, and hooked them up to the buggy. Then he got in and without a glance my way drove back up the short street.

Stepping into the saddle, I walked the roan up to the general store and went in. I bought myself a sack of Arbuckle's coffee and some cartridges. The man who waited on me looked at me, noticing the back of my head. "Looks like you've been wounded."

"Scratch," I said. I was looking out the window at the buggy. Clinton had come out and put his valise in the back, and after a minute or two, Janet came out. She looked up an' down the street like she was looking for somebody or maybe for a way out.

Clinton took off his hat and approached her, and she smiled and accepted his hand to get into the buggy. I paid for the goods I'd bought and never so much as looked at my change.

"She's a pretty girl," the clerk commented.

"That she is, and she's in damn bad company."

"My uncle, he's the owner here, agrees with you. He knew Clinton in Denver."

"Yeah?"

"He killed a man there over a card game, and was pretty well known around Laramie Street. My uncle recognized him when he first rode into town. Says he's a bad actor. Very quick with a gun, and mean."

"Thanks. I'll remember."

"You're Mr. Passin', aren't you? Passin' Through?"

"That's what they call me."

"A man named Reed Bell was in a few days ago. He said he'd missed you around but to warn you. He said to tell you you were a poor judge of age."

"He did, did he? Thanks." Starting for the door, I turned back. "If he comes in, you tell him I'm riding out to the ranch. That it looks like there's going to be a settlement."

"I haven't seen him this week. He may have left the country."

"Not if he's a better judge of age than I am. You just tell him."

When I walked outside they were just driving away. Alongside his broad shoulders she looked almighty small and lonesome. I put my packets into my saddlebags and climbed aboard. I had a bad feeling about all this, a mighty bad feeling.

To tell you the truth, I was scared. Janet Le Caudy was walking right into a kind of trouble she might never get out of, without any real appreciation of what she was facing. Most people have no understanding or expectation of violence. They read of it in newspapers or books but it doesn't touch them. They've no realization of how vicious and murderous some people can be, or what they are prepared to do for money. And it did not have to be a lot of money.

On a cattle outfit where I worked, a man was killed in an argument over a rawhide quirt that wasn't worth three dollars, and I'd seen another man killed in a saloon in Ogallala because when he turned to spit he missed the cuspidor and hit a man's polished boot.

The thought hit me so sudden I pulled up on my horse and the roan stopped in its tracks. Ogallala, and I'd come in there with a cattle drive where I was trail boss, with twenty-five hundred head of Texas longhorns and sixteen riders to handle them.

The town was wide open and kicking up its heels, with maybe twenty thousand head of cattle grazing on the grass outside of town and all their riders ready to get paid off so they could come in a-shootin'. And some had already been paid. I was nineteen if I recalled correctly, and not many of those riders were more than five years older or younger. They were chock-full of vinegar and they would have money to spend.

Ogallala's legitimate businessmen were there aplenty, but the drifting gamblers, the women from the Line and their fancy men, the con men an' crossroaders, they were all there, nostrils dilated with the smell of money.

The cowboys were young, they'd been fighting stampedes, hailstorms, dust storms, and occasional Indians all the way from Texas. Every man jack of them had eaten a few pounds of dust and had ridden across a small corner of hell. They were ready for some fun, anything to break the monotony of what they were doing. The only saving grace to all that hard work was that they could do it a-horseback. And I was one of them, only a boss, which made it different. I was responsible for the cattle and for them.

So I remembered that shooting. It had not been one of my boys but a rider from one of the Ab Blocker herds, or so I thought. He was seventeen and a good lad, riding, I'd heard, his second drive over the trail. And now he was dead because he'd spit on somebody's boot.

Two of my boys had come into the saloon with me and I just said, "Back off, boys, just back off now. This isn't our fight."

They backed off, but I had an idea what would happen when the boys who rode with him heard of it. They'd come a-foggin' it.

Somebody spoke up and said, "That man you killed is only one of a very tough outfit. They've two herds outside of town and twenty-nine Texas cowhands. You don't want to be here when they come huntin' you. I'd suggest Rapid City or Deadwood or Bismarck."

"I can't—"

The man speaking was the saloonkeeper, and he lifted a sawed-off shotgun from behind the bar. "Those women of yours will get along without you, but I'm not goin' to have my saloon shot up because of some cold-blooded—"

The killer turned and looked at him. "When this is over I'll come back lookin' for you."

"Anytime"—the saloonkeeper rolled his cigar in his teeth—"but you'd better see me first."

The killer turned and went out of the saloon and a few

minutes later he was riding out of town. We could hear the horse, and the saloonkeeper put his shotgun back under the bar.

I remembered the scene, remembered it well, and now I had more reason to remember because that killer who had ridden out of town was a man I now remembered.

His name was Charles Pelham Clinton.

EIGHTEEN

So now I had no choice. Like it or not I had to ride over to the ranch and be sure that Janet got out of there alive.

Before this I had believed I knew the kind of man he was, now I was sure. But what was his connection with Matty and Mrs. Hollyrood? Or was there a connection? Why was he getting involved at all? And why had Matty warned me away? Why had she advised me not to eat a meal or have a drink with them? Especially when I already had eaten many meals, and well-cooked ones, too. It didn't seem to make any kind of sense.

This time I rode due west from town, not wanting to retrace any trail I'd previously ridden, riding down the draw back of the house. The draw I'd ridden before, but not the first part of the trail.

Before reaching the draw I rode at a spanking good trot, anxious to reach the place about the same time they arrived in the buggy. I was tying my horse to a cedar when the buggy pulled up outside. It needed only minutes to get down to the house, and as there was a window open I could hear what was said.

"Mrs. Hollyrood? This is Janet Le Caudy. I believe she has a claim on this ranch."

"Do sit down, my dear. Do we have to talk business right away? Matty, have you made coffee? Then let me." I could hear her cross the room, heard her fussing with dishes as she talked.

"There is so much confusion about this, when there need not be," Mrs. Hollyrood was saying. "We presented our papers and there was no objection. The judge recognized our claim was valid."

"I am afraid, Mrs. Hollyrood, that whatever judge you met with did not have all the facts. You see, my uncle did not own the ranch outright. Half of it is in my name."

She turned, I could see her plainly now. That she was shocked was obvious. "Mr. Phillips did not own it? How could that be?"

"Simply that half of the ranch has always been mine, and of course he understood that. The ownership had never been in question, and I cannot imagine him writing a will that would leave property he did not own."

There was silence in the room. Then Clinton said, "Now you see the situation, Dory. It was a nice try but you did not have all the facts."

At Clinton's use of her first name I saw Janet give him a quick, startled glance. "Dory"? I had not heard the first name myself, but it spoke of some familiarity between them. Matty was standing back, watching.

"It's no problem, dear. I am sure Miss Le Caudy and I can reach an agreement. After all, a pretty young girl shouldn't have to worry about all this property. And running a ranch? With *cattle*? She wouldn't think of it."

"On the contrary," Janet spoke quietly, "I have always wished to live on a ranch, and I like working with cattle. Besides"— she was very cool, and now must realize something of the situation—"I have hoped to get Mr. Passin' to manage the place for me."

"You know Passin'?" Mrs. Hollyrood glanced at Clinton. "You did not tell me that, Pell."

"They've talked, that's all."

"Oh, we talked quite a lot!" Janet was using her head now. "He didn't want me to come out here, and I am beginning to believe he was right." She stood up. "Mr. Clinton? If you will be so good as to drive me back to town?"

"Please, Miss Le Caudy. Or shall I just call you Janet? Do sit down. Whatever difficulties we have can be arranged. There's nothing to worry about, nothing at all. A good hot cup of coffee will make us all feel better. Just you sit down, now. Matty? Is there any of that cake left? Please get it down. I know Janet would like something with her coffee."

If Janet was frightened she offered no evidence of it. By now she knew there was some understanding between Clinton and

Dory Hollyrood. She would also be remembering that Clinton had her leave the hotel with all her belongings. Nobody now knew where she was but Passin'.

"Put out enough cake for one more." Janet was calm. "Mr. Passin' will be coming out, I am sure."

"Pell?" Dory Hollyrood's tone was sharp. "You said Pan would handle that. You promised."

"And so he will, you can be sure."

Janet smiled. She was seated at the end of the table and I could see her clearly. "Pan, did you say? Would that be Pan Beacham? Isn't he some sort of a hired killer?"

There was a dead silence in the room and then Matty spoke. "I think we're in trouble. I think we should all ride out of here now, while we still can."

"Don't be a fool!" Mrs. Hollyrood snapped. "And you stay out of this. You're not a part of it."

She turned to Clinton. "You told me she was young and a fool. For a man of your experience you can be very gullible."

Mrs. Hollyrood turned to Janet. "Where did you hear of Pan Beacham?"

She shrugged a shoulder. "Doesn't everyone know about him? People out here talk about gunfighters the way we talk about actors, politicians, or prizefighters back east. Everybody knows about Pan Beacham."

"I believe," Matty put in again, "we should get in that buggy and drive to the railroad. I think we should go now."

"Stay out of this, Matty!" Dory Hollyrood's tone was sharp. "You're not in this."

"You can't get away with it," Matty said. "If there ever was a time when you could, that time is past. I believe we should leave, and right now."

"Don't be silly! There's nothing to be alarmed about. So Miss Le Caudy owns half the ranch? That's very simple. She will sign it over to us." He smiled. "For a consideration, of course."

"It can be discussed at the proper time. Now, Mr. Clinton, I really would like to return to Parrott City."

Nobody paid any attention to her, and I could see she was trying to make up her mind as to her next move. She could get up and walk out but that would simply force an issue that might offer another solution. I slipped the thong off my six-shooter and glanced around quickly. There was nobody else around, nobody I could see.

Matty persisted. "You'd better listen. She said Mr. Passin' will be coming out."

"Nonsense!" Mrs. Hollyrood started to say something else, then stopped. "Did he tell you he was coming?"

"He will be, if I know him," she said, "and I think I do. I should have listened to him then." She looked at Clinton. "I trusted you."

Clinton smiled. "People often do. It is an advantage." He turned to Mrs. Hollyrood. "Dory, don't worry about him. Pan will handle that."

Janet ignored the coffee that was placed before her, but the table had been set and she glanced down at the knife and fork. I hoped she was thinking what I was thinking. "I believe you are mistaken in trusting so much to this Pan you speak of. I don't believe he could understand the kind of man Mr. Passin' is."

"He doesn't need to understand." Clinton smiled. "He just operates."

"My father always said it paid to understand one's enemies." She looked up at Clinton. "Your Mr. Pan evidently made a mistake."

There was another dead silence, then Clinton looked over at her. "Just what do you mean, Pan made a mistake?"

"I would call it that. He tried to kill Mr. Passin'."

She was obviously enjoying herself. She was in danger, and she knew it now. She knew the kind of people she was dealing with and she knew they did not intend for her to live, so she was playing every card, trying to undermine their confidence in themselves, in their plan, if they had one. The more I listened the more I believed they were just cheap, clumsy murderers who had killed a man, faked a will, then claimed the ranch, all with too little information. Now they would try to cover their mistakes with more murder.

Clinton was bothered. He leaned his knuckles on the table. "What do you mean he 'tried'?"

"Just that."

"What happened?"

"I don't know exactly, except that Pan Beacham isn't with us anymore."

Again there was silence. When Clinton spoke again his voice

was shaking. "You're lying, damn you! You're lying! Nobody could beat Pan! He was the best! He never took a chance!"

Janet, pale and quiet, sat very still. Her right hand was close to the table knife. "I believe," she spoke quietly, "you had better drive me into town. Or give me a horse and I'll ride. I think you should realize that you're through here, all through."

"Like hell!"

"Your luck's run out," she persisted. "You can't go against that. From the beginning everything has gone wrong for you. If you persist you will wind up hanging.

"Let me go, and get out of here as fast as you can."

"I think she's right," Matty said.

"Shut up!" Mrs. Hollyrood's tone was hoarse. "Keep out of this!"

"Nobody could beat Pan," Clinton repeated sullenly. "You're lying!"

Again I looked around, looked around carefully. There was nobody in sight, not much of any place for anybody to hide, close up. I was hoping she would talk her way out of it, although I hadn't much hope. So far she'd been uncommonly cool. Scared, yes, but handling it better than most and trying to use every chip she had, which wasn't much.

Their efforts had been a botched-up mess from the beginning. Most murderers were people of low intelligence no matter what their income or their station in life, and murder was a difficult thing to hide.

A lonely old man had taken her to dinner a few times and no doubt talked with enthusiasm about his ranch. Knowing little of ranches and not realizing Phillips' enthusiasm for his place, she had pictured it far different than it was. She made her plans, with or without help from Matty or Clinton, had murdered Phillips, and then come west to take over the ranch, using a forged will.

They had, because he seemed to be alone, assumed he had no relatives. He might even have said he had no wife or children. Arriving, they had found the ranch less than expected. It was a good ranch, but it needed to be worked and work was no part of their planning. Mrs. Hollyrood had then decided to sell. Perhaps she even had ideas of murdering me for whatever I carried, be it a few hundred or a few thousand dollars. Most criminals are optimists. They have to be. They have to believe in their projects and they convince themselves everybody else is stupid. Why else would a person risk several years in prison for a few dollars? It never made sense to me.

Now they had planned to murder Janet. To get her out here — where nobody could say what happened, and where she would not be expected back by anyone. Her possessions gone from the hotel, they would assume she had gone about her business.

At first my help must have seemed important, just doing work they did not wish to do. Then I'd gotten that tally book, and looking into the drawer Mrs. Hollyrood must have seen a stain where something else had been. Naturally suspicious, she began to wonder. And then they had decided to kill me. I simply knew too much and was becoming dangerous. Actually, I knew very little.

"You could go now," Janet was saying. "You could get over the county line and keep going. Nobody would find you and I doubt if they'd keep looking for long."

Somehow I had to get her out of there alive. How to do it was the question. Clinton was good with a gun, and he'd be in a panic and liable to start shooting. In a case like that, Janet could get shot very easily. I had to get her out of there and away.

At any time one of them might decide to make a move and do so without warning. They had about talked themselves out. If they started to move, I would act, but there should be a better way.

Janet had offered them a way out, but she should realize that if they took it they would murder her first, to leave no witness, nobody to set the police on them.

Who else might ask a question? There was only me. And they would think of that, too.

But I was a drifter, and nobody might listen. The solution they came to would always be the one they wanted to find.

"All right." Clinton's tone was resigned. "You're right, of course. We'll have something to eat and then I'll drive you into Parrott."

He looked up. "Matty? Will you fix something?"

"Don't bother, Matty." Dory Hollyrood was on her feet. "You go to your room. I'll do it."

Matty hesitated and seemed about to speak, but before she could say what was on her mind, Mrs. Hollyrood said, more sharply, "Matty? Go to your room!"

Matty turned and without a word went up the stairs.

Janet pushed back a little from the table. "Can I help?" she asked.

"No, honey, you sit right there. We'll have something together in no time.

"I always did like to fuss around in a kitchen," she said. "Folks wouldn't be likely to think that was so, with me being an actress, and all.

"That's the trouble with being on the road, a person doesn't get a chance to cook, fix up, or sew. You never really have a home to go to.

"I'm sorry," she added, "that we got into this little mix-up. It hasn't been as bad as it sounds, and I am sure poor Mr. Phillips made some kind of mistake. You get to thinking about it and you will understand.

"He was a kindly man. Liked to do things for folks. Evidently when he wrote that will leaving everything to me, he forgot about anybody else for the moment. If he had lived he would have made things right.

"You say you like a ranch, and ranch life? Well, you just keep the ranch. We'll go back to show business, Matty and me. Of course, we could do with a little traveling money, so I'd sell my share to you for whatever you can offer. We'll just put it down to a mistake by poor Mr. Phillips."

As she chattered, she was working. Her fingers were quick, and she seemed to know where everything was.

"There now! We'll have things ready in a minute. You drink up your coffee now—"

"I'm afraid it's gotten cold."

"Now, now! Cold coffee's not all that bad! You just drink up!"

"If you like cold coffee," Janet said, smiling, "drink this. I haven't so much as touched it."

Clinton looked over at Mrs. Hollyrood. "She knows," he said.

At that moment I heard a faint sound from above. Matty was in the window on the second floor. She was looking down at me.

NINETEEN

Our eyes met and for a moment they held, then she with-drew her head, and I waited, but nothing happened. My eyes returned to the scene within.

"She knows," Clinton repeated.

"I only know that I wish to return to my hotel." Janet was on her feet. "I believe our lawyers can handle this better than we. Evidently," she added, "my uncle's memory seemed to have failed him. We had always been very friendly partners, and it was my understanding that when he died I was to have his share also."

"Sit down," Mrs. Hollyrood said. "We are not through."

Janet remained standing. "I believe we are." She was very cool but I could see that she was frightened, and they could see it also.

How could it be otherwise? She was alone, far from town, and with two people whom she must by now realize were murderers. Phillips would not have forgotten his "beloved niece," so the will they had must be forged.

"We will write a bill of sale," Clinton said, "and when you sign it, you can go."

"I do not believe Mr. Passin' would advise it," Janet said. She was alert, ready to move. What she had in mind I'd no idea, but she was ready, ready for anything that offered a way out.

"Your Mr. Passin' is not here. There's nothing he could do if he was. It is all up to you now. To you, and to us. After all"— Clinton smiled—"it's just land, and you're young. Why risk a life that is so young?"

She smiled back. "You may be right. My aunt told me I

wouldn't like it here. In fact, we have a little wager. She offered to bet I would be back in Durango within ten days. That"—she was lying coolly—"was nine days ago. She will be expecting me to be here when they ride out to see me."

"She's lying!" Mrs. Hollyrood said irritably. "Can't you see she's making it all up?"

Charles Pelham Clinton hesitated. He was beginning to like this less and less. I could see it in his manner.

"Suppose she isn't? Suppose this aunt of hers rides out to see her?"

Dory Hollyrood was impatient. She got out a tablet and a pen and ink. "Pell? Write it out. She'll sign it if she knows what's good for her."

Clinton hesitated, then sat down. Taking up the pen, he started to write. He was at the opposite end of the table from Janet and she was standing. Suddenly she stooped slightly and shoved hard on the table.

She moved so swiftly her action was totally unexpected. The end of the table smashed against Clinton's breastbone, and the bench upon which he was sitting went over backward, spilling him to the floor in a tangle of chair, table, and his legs. With almost the same movement Janet threw the coffee, cup and all, at Dory Hollyrood, then she was out of the door.

It caught me flatfooted as well. Then I was around the corner of the house. "Janet! This way!"

She had hesitated, not knowing which way was safest. Instantly she came to me.

From inside there was an angry scream. "Pell! *Get* her!"

We were running back toward my horse and I had jerked the slipknot when two men stepped from the shadow of the oaks.

The nearest one was Lew Paine, as I knew the voice. He said, "Now I've got you, you—!"

He always had to shoot off his mouth.

I shot off my gun.

Runnin' like that, I was all keyed up, an' when he spoke I just naturally hauled iron and let him have it. The other man turned to run and fell on the rocks. He had sense enough to lay still and I let him lay. Clinton was coming from the house, and whilst I might have gotten aboard and away, there was no time for the two of us on the same horse, so we ducked into the brush.

Clinton came up, a rifle in his hands. "Who's that? What happened?"

Somebody groaned, and I guess it was Paine. The other man said, "I dunno. He come out a-foggin' it an' when Lew spoke he just let him have it."

Clinton swore. The blue roan had walked off a few steps and was standing, ears up, head lifted.

"Where'd he go?" Clinton demanded.

"Into the brush." The speaker got to his feet. "There was somebody with him."

"Kill him tonight and I'll give you a hundred dollars," Clinton said. "Cash on the barrelhead."

"No, sir, you won't. I might kill a man because I was mad or to help a friend, like Lew here, but not for money." He hitched up his belt. "Anyway, this here's one old he-coon. I wouldn't go back in that brush after him for a gold mine. If you want him dead, you go make him that way yourself.

"Anyway," he added, "I got Lew to think of. I gotta get help for him. I think he's bad hurt."

Clinton swore, then walked back to the house. Very gently I lifted a foot, felt for a good place, and put it down. Janet followed.

We were out on a hillside where there was some brush and in the distance a forest of ponderosa. Our only chance to hide was to merge with the small trees and brush, and there was no good place to be.

Where was the roan? It had walked off somewhere and my eyes failed to pick it out of the darkness. Gently, I took another step, letting my foot down slowly until it held my weight, then moving the other. I didn't want him shooting at sound. He might hit one of us, and in his frame of mind he might just start firing into the darkness.

They would be desperate now, but desperate or not, they would be cautious. Pan Beacham, Janet had told them, was dead. That would be warning enough for Clinton.

That fool Paine! My guess was that he'd had enough, but something led him back there and he believed he had me dead to rights. Why couldn't he have left well enough alone? Had he not reentered the picture, Janet and I would be riding double on the roan and halfway to Parrott.

My head was aching again and I was tired, wanting nothing so much as just to lie down. We moved on, a step at a time.

When we managed to get about fifty yards away, keeping quiet, we just began to walk. If we could reach the road just before it got to the ranch house, we might catch some late traveler.

After a bit I said, "I've got to sit down. I'm all in."

We both sat down and I said, "I was shot a while back. Lost blood."

"I know. Pan Beacham, wasn't it?"

"It was. He come on me in the mountains, thought he had me dead to rights."

"But you killed him?"

"He was comin' after me. Didn't leave me much choice." I paused. "He had some connection with them."

"So I gathered."

We sat quiet then, and I even dozed a little. Then she touched my arm, gently. "Something is coming!" she whispered.

That opened my eyes. Listening, I heard nothing. Then a faint sound of movement, something brushing through leaves. I stood up, shucking my pistol.

More movement, then the sound of a horse moving. Suddenly, I knew what it was. "Come on," I spoke softly, "come on over."

It was the roan.

"How did he find us?" Janet whispered.

"Some horses can follow a trail like a houn' dog. The wild ones are best at it, but mostly they follow other horses."

I rubbed his neck and talked to him. "We'll get out of here now," I said. "This is a good strong horse and he can carry double, for a ways, anyway."

Parrott was the place to go. Back to where there was people and I could get Janet into some kind of safety. Me, I was going to leave the country. With all this shooting, nobody would be wanting any part of me. The days for that sort of thing had about passed, and folks just didn't want it happening.

The rest had made me feel better, and I'd always been quick to recover. When a man spends his life with hard work in the fresh air in this mountain country, it takes a lot to kill him.

Things were quiet when we rode back into town, and as nobody new had come in, Janet was able to get her room back. The man who was the law around here had ridden into Animas City so I went back to the restaurant and the man I knew.

Nobody was in. "Come out and sit with me," I said, "I've some talkin' to do."

He took a good look at me and came with two cups and a pot of Arbuckle's. Taking the will from my pocket, I showed it to him. "That ranch belongs to Janet Le Caudy," I said. "Half of it was hers, anyway. My guess is that Dory Hollyrood poisoned Phillips, forged a will or had her fancy man do it, and then she came out here figuring she'd gotten herself a real stylish layout.

"She surely didn't find what she expected, and then she began talkin' about sellin' out. Then Janet showed up with a claim." I laid it all out for him. "She'll be in, you can talk to her."

"Why tell me? I'm not the law."

"You're somebody who knows us. You know us a little bit, anyway, and I want the facts on record. That woman," I added, "is mean. I figure she planned to poison me for my stake. It isn't much but she'll settle for whatever she can get."

"You'd better talk to Reed Bell."

"The Pink? Is he still around?"

"Been in an' out all day, askin' for you." The cook grinned. "He said not to trust you."

"Not to trust me? Why?"

"He said not to trust you at guessin' a woman's age."

I shrugged. "With a horse you can look at their teeth, just try doin' that to a woman." I looked over my cup at him. "Where'd I miss on that?"

"He didn't say, but—he's comin' across the street now."

Bell came in, put his hat down on the table, and ran his fingers through what hair he had left. "You're a hard man to keep track of, Passin'," he said, "I never did see a man keep moving so much."

"I kep' my hair. I mean, nobody took my scalp."

"I've been scatterin' around some my own self. You said that Mrs. Hollyrood was an actress?"

"That's what she told me. Showed me some old playbills, too."

"Oh, she's been an actress, all right. A lot else, too. She still at the ranch?"

"So far's I know. They may cut an' run now that we got away from them." I cleared my throat. "I had a shootin' with Lew Paine."

"He's been askin' for it. The sheriff will probably give you a vote of thanks. Sooner or later he would have had to do it."

"He's alive. He come on me sudden an' he was standin' with brush in the background an' my shot was too quick."

"That Mrs. Hollyrood? You sent me off on a blind trail. You said she was fifty, sixty years old, if I recall?"

"She must be. She's got gray hair, an'—"

"Ever hear of anybody wearin' a wig? That's what she's got. Three or four of them, as a matter of fact. To tell you the truth, she's in her middle thirties, somewhere. And she's got dark hair when it's natural, which it rarely is."

"You going to arrest her?"

"Uh-huh. Soon as the sheriff gets back."

"Clinton, too?"

"Charles Pelham Clinton, know the man well. No, we just don't have evidence enough. Maybe if you and Miss Le Caudy make a statement—"

"We will, but I don't think we have much that would stand up in court."

Later, I went across the street and got a room for myself, then I hunted up the town barber and treated myself to a haircut and a shave, changed my clothes, and then stretched out on the bed to catch forty winks, as the saying is.

When I opened my eyes again it was full dark. Looking out the window, I couldn't see a light in town. The restaurant was dark and nobody was moving around, so I just undressed and went back to bed.

It was a few minutes before I went back to sleep, and lying there I wondered what was happening at the ranch and what Mrs. Hollyrood would do now. Most of all I wondered about Matty. She was caught up in something she should get shut of before they decided she knew too much and wasn't loyal enough. Of course, they did not know that she'd seen me outside the house nor that she had warned me away before that.

"Mr. Passin'," I said to myself, "you got yourself into a lot that didn't concern you. Now you'd better saddle up, pack up, and hit the trail for the high-up hills."

Another thing was naggin' at me. Here I was, twenty-eight years old with a lot of rough country behind me, and all I had in the world was three horses, a rope, some mining tools, and a few shootin' irons that I was having to clean all the time.

Right now, due to a streak of luck in hitting that pocket of ore, I had more money than ever in my life before, but when a man came right down to it the little I had didn't amount to much, and when that was gone, what was left? A job punching cows at thirty bucks a month or back to prospecting? Suddenly I began to feel I didn't want to spend my years looking a burro in the behind while I followed him over the mountains.

I sat up, put my hat on, and folded my arms around my knees. Somehow I always think better with my hat on.

Then another uneasy feeling came over me. Why, all of a sudden, was I thinking like this? Why, after all those rambling years, was I suddenly beginning to think like a taxpayer?

I'd been telling myself for years that I was a mean man, and there were some who would agree. Here and there I'd been hard to get along with, mostly because I don't take to getting pushed around, but all the while other men I'd ridden with had their own ranches, opened banks, I mean, legitimately, or had become lawyers or storekeepers. I mean, they were *citizens*. What was I but a saddle tramp?

Well, I took my hat off and lay back down and stared at the ceiling, feeling uneasy with myself. All right, I was twenty-eight. Where was I going to be when I was forty? Still riding the rough string for some other man?

When somebody wanted to know who I was, would I have to say I was just Passin' Through?

Well, that's what we all were doing, in a way, but when a man cashes in his chips he should leave something a little better than he had found it.

Matty now, Matty should get shut of those people. It was my feeling she had fallen in with them and was about to get herself into trouble through misguided loyalty. Sometimes a person gets to running with the wrong crowd and stays with them even when he knows he shouldn't. Maybe it's because he doesn't know anybody else or because it's become a habit. There had been a few times when I was younger that I had traipsed around with folks I'd sort of fallen in with, folks who, if I hadn't left them, would surely have gotten me hung.

There was that Texas outfit, a wild bunch, but not a good wild bunch, if you know what I mean. They weren't just blowing off steam like cowhands often do, there was a meanness to what they did. One night they started talking of holding up a train and I listened, and when we rode off to our separate places that night I just kept riding, clean out of the country. I'd been sixteen then, man-grown and rugged, but with an ounce of brains picked up from somewhere. There were six in the outfit until I rode off and left them. They held up their train, all right, and when they split up the take, each man got twenty-six dollars and fifty cents. A year later two of them, showing less brains than I'd have expected, tried to hold up a stage on which Eugene Blair was riding shotgun. Those boys aren't with us anymore. Another was in prison, and two were hung by impatient citizens.

Tomorrow was another day, and when I fell asleep I was remembering the rope I'd had around my own neck.

TWENTY

First morning in my life when I'd been in bed past seven o'clock, but when I awoke I was rested for the first time in weeks. For a few minutes I just lay there thinking how good it felt, then I got up, shaved, and dressed. All the time I was conscious of what was happening in the street below, and whilst shaving could glance from the corners of my eyes up the street toward the tall building, all of two stories, that ended the street. Back of it the La Platas lifted toward the sky. No snow on them yet, but it wouldn't be many weeks.

From the Dutchman's blacksmith shop I could hear the clang of his hammer on the anvil where he was shoeing a horse or sharpening steel for some miner.

Up Deadwood Gulch where the aspens were turning to gold I could see the smoke from a chimney, vaguely blue against the pines.

Slinging my gun around my hips, I tried to think back to a day when I hadn't worn one. Ninety percent of the men down there in the street would be armed, but those days were passing. Would I pass with them? I shook my head to rid it of such thoughts. It was a wild and rough west we had come into and it needed men with the bark on.

By the time I reached the street, most men were at work. The morning sun was pleasant and I loafed along the street in front of the general store. A youngster came out with a small striped paper sack of candy in his hand. When I was his age most candy still had medicinal centers, but that was already passing off in the cities. A woman went into the door and when I went in she was buying some dress goods. Most women made their own clothes and a woman who couldn't sew was a rarity.

141

The clerk was showing her a bolt of cloth, had it spread out on the counter. I walked across the room to look at a saddle, all carved leather and fancy, like no saddle a workin' cowhand could afford, although most times the saddles were worth more than the horse who carried it.

Idling around, looking at some spurs, some fancy, some workaday types, and ropes. Me, I always made my own riatas out of rawhide the way the Mexicans did. In fact it was an old Mex showed me the way of it. The best ropers around were the Californios or Mexicans, most of them using ropes twice as long as the average workin' cowboy whom I knew.

Truth was, I was kind of watching for Janet. I figured she would be on her way to the restaurant pretty soon and maybe I could get to eat with her again. Not that she'd have much use for me now that the trouble was over. I walked back to the street, hating to leave the wonderful smells of that general store, fresh ground coffee (they got the beans in big burlap bags and ground them on the premises), new leather, and dry goods.

There wasn't much happening in the stores. The men had gone to work and most women were about their household work and wouldn't be coming to shop for a couple of hours yet, maybe more.

The Dutchman had quit work and was walking across to the restaurant for coffee. There were a couple of strange horses tied to the hitch rail in front of a saloon.

At the distance I could not make out the brands, but then I didn't know much about the brands in this part of the country.

A few clouds were showing in the blue sky. I walked across the street, paused in the door of the restaurant to look around, then went inside. It was a mighty peaceful time, so why should I be feeling uneasy?

The Dutchman was at his coffee and he nodded to me. Most folks knew who I was by now. News gets around quick in a small town, and I could see folks stealing glances at me but nobody seemed anxious to talk. They'd heard about Houston Burrows and even Pan Beacham and my brief difficulty with Lew Paine, so I was trouble.

The Dutchman, a hardworking man, probably felt the same, although he knew I hadn't much choice. "You kill Beacham?"

"Left me no choice. He come for me."

The Dutchman's mug of coffee looked like a thimble in his

hand, it was that big. "I know him. Bad man." He gulped coffee and broke a piece from the corn pone before him. "I know him in Trinidad. He is brother to Clinton."

Well, now! That explained some things but left the gate wide open for trouble.

He looked over at me. "You bring much trouble with you. You go soon?"

Irritation began to mount in me, and I liked the Dutchman. He was a good man. He worked hard and was good at what he did.

"Probably," I said. "I'd like to see Miss Le Caudy get settled on her ranch first. She's had a lot of trouble."

They knew that to be true and they knew that I had ridden point for her in all of it.

That was well and good. They knew what I had done and why I had done it but that was over now. Trouble had a way of building around a man who was known to be good with a gun, and they did not want trouble. The west was growing up and they no longer liked the old wild cowboy reputation. The railroad had come in, Animas City was giving way to Durango, and they were thinking of being a city. They wished to attract businessmen, not the wild bunch. We who rode the lone trails, our time was running out.

Businessmen were showing their irritation by coming out and shooting some of the wild bunch out of their saddles. The unknowing were too quick to forget that most of those businessmen had been soldiers in the Civil and Indian wars, and many had been cattlemen themselves. They knew just as much about guns and fighting as did the outlaws, and in some cases a good deal more.

The Lincoln County War down New Mexico way had fought itself out, and only last July, not sixty days ago, Billy the Kid had been killed at Fort Sumner by Pat Garrett.

"Two mens come this day, very early." The Dutchman was talking to me. "They come from the west. I do not know them, and they do not talk." He swallowed some coffee. "They look at your horses. They talk about the roan, and I think they know him. I think they know that horse."

Only half my mind was following him. I was watching for Janet and she was not coming. Or had she already gone? I wished to ask but did not. Both of these men would know.

I rode a blue horse to where the trails divided, and the blue horse brought me here.

"Will you stay?" The Dutchman was persistent.

He wished to be rid of me. No animosity, just because he did not think me good for the town or the time. I smiled at him. "Right now, Dutch, I don't know. I'm thinking of taking my outfit and riding up the mountains to where the rivers are born. I'm thinking of going up there to look for whatever I can find. I'm a looker and a seeker, Dutchman, not a man who hunts trouble.

"None of this that's been happening was of my choosing. They came to me and I accommodated them to clear the road for the settling of that ranch. When Janet Le Caudy is settled and safe I will ride on."

"We take care of her."

Well, I looked at him. "Dutch, you've got drills to sharpen, hinges to make, and horses to shoe. Will you be sitting on her ranch if Charles Pelham Clinton comes back? Could you handle him if he did come? I mean, with a gun?"

"I think it better you go."

"Give me time, Dutchman, give me time."

Getting up, I walked outside. There were two men down the street, standing together. There was another across the street standing by the horses, and it all looked natural enough except that it was the middle of the morning and few men loafed about at that hour.

Up in my room I stretched out on the bed but I did not sleep. "You've got to ride away, Mr. Passin'," I said to myself. "You've got to find a place where nobody knows you. Particularly you've got to ride away before that trouble down the street begins to happen."

They were through with me here. I'd worn out my welcome. If I rode out of town those men would follow and they would all be rid of me.

I stared up at the ceiling, suddenly lonely, sad for myself, and wondering what the next step would be. Would those men even let me get out of town? Or would it happen down there? And who were they, anyway? Maybe it was somebody else they wanted? Yet I knew it was me. I knew they wanted me in their sights and they had what they believed was a reason.

Maybe I was like Matty, only she was worse off, being a woman. I doubted if she had any money, being dependent on

Mrs. Hollyrood, and she was too beautiful, with no home, no relatives, no place to go. Some of that I knew, some I had surmised. To get a job she would have to work for a man, and the man, chances were, would have a wife. Few wives would want to have so beautiful a woman working day after day with their husbands, even as still, cold, and quiet a woman as Matty.

When sundown came I went across the street to eat. When I glanced down the street only one man was there, loitering in front of a saloon and smoking a cigarette. Well, they were going to get their chance. I'd be no more trouble to Parrott. When the night came I would get my horses and ride out, and whatever those men were after they would find. They'd find it somewhere on down the trail, and I hoped they'd be satisfied with what they found.

Cook didn't have much to say until he'd served my meal and two other customers had gone. Then he brought the coffeepot and sat down across from me. "Sorry about that," he said, "sorry about this mornin', but the Dutchman was speakin' for the community."

"You, too?"

"No, not me. I told them you were a good man to have around, but they wouldn't buy it. Things had been quiet, they said, until you came. They want you gone. The Dutchman feels like me but they asked him to speak for them."

"I'll ride out tonight."

"Sorry to see you go." He paused. "The Dutchman will get your horses, saddle up for you, load your pack. Why don't you go up the canyon? You can ride over the rim and down Bear Creek. They'll never know what happened to you."

"I never got anywhere sidestepping trouble."

"This time you'd better. If you want there's a trail up the side of the canyon, up Madden. If you want to go west you could follow the Mancos down. If I were you I'd ride out Bear Creek. There's something doing at a place called Telluride. I've never been there myself."

"I don't follow the camps. I like wild country."

"You'll find it."

We were silent then, and others came in, ate, and left. It was time I was leaving.

"If you're thinking of the young lady," cook said, "she left on the stage for Durango. Pulled out this morning. Seems she's got another aunt in there. The aunt's not a resident. She came out to try to get her niece to come home with her."

"Think she'll do it?"

"Why not? A ranch like that is no place for a young, pretty girl. Too lonesome. She'll go back east, I reckon."

"Was she in here?"

"Early this morning, about daylight. Ate her breakfast and seemed in no hurry."

My cup was empty. I stared into it, then got up slowly. "All right," I said, "if the Dutchman will bring my horses to the upper end of town, I'll ride out."

"Back of the courthouse," Cookie said. "That's what they call it," he added.

It wasn't like me to slip out of town, ducking trouble, but this was the way they wanted it. A half-hour later I'd come out of the back door of the hotel and walked up back of the buildings to where the Dutchman waited.

"T'ank you, Mr. Passin'," he said. "I know this not your way, but if it keeps the peace—"

I stepped into the saddle. "See you sometime, Dutchman. No hard feelings."

That night I made a fireless camp on the side of Parrott Peak, but well back in the timber. When day came, without eating breakfast, I crossed over the ridge, then the saddle between Helmet Peak and the Hogback, and camped again in Echo Basin. When morning came I followed down the creek until it joined the West Mancos River, and found some men working a prospect. They were just finishing breakfast so I sat down with them.

"You're ridin' a high-country and a lonely trail," one said. "Prospectin'?"

"Not this trip, but I've done some." Gesturing toward my pack, I said, "I'm geared up for it but right now I thought I'd head for Silverton."

"Last night," another commented, "I was over on Burnt Ridge and I could see a campfire down at T-Down Park. I had my glasses and I could make out three men. No packhorses. Seemed to be ridin' light." He looked at me again. "They wouldn't be lookin' to meet you, would they?"

"That might be their intention. It isn't mine. However, if they catch up to me, I'll try to entertain them."

We talked about color, outcroppings, and plants that might

indicate minerals. I told them about pockets I'd found and they told me of their present discovery. Then I got up. "Thanks for the beans," I said. "If you ever ride up to a camp of mine, you're welcome."

"If we do," one said, "we'll ride careful." He paused. "Three can be quite a few."

"But one can be too many," I agreed.

They were bright boys, those men on my trail. They had figured it right. Somehow I'd gotten out of town, and not toward the stage route or the ranch. La Plata Canyon was a possibility, but either they had information, which I doubted, or they had guessed right, and now they were only a few miles away. So far they were guessing, but they might have a clue. I got into the Gold Run Trail and rode it down to the Lost Canyon Stock Driveway. They were going to find me and there was no use running, but I'd try. There were three of them and one of me, and they could spread out and signal with a rifle shot when one sighted me.

Riding just below timberline, I halted at every possible spot to look over the country and to listen. Sound carries quite a distance in the high country, but I figured they were below me, and I should hear them before I saw them.

Drawing my rifle from the scabbard, I rode carefully. My heart was pounding. Three tough men, but who *were* they?

This was big, big country, but not so easy to lose one's self in because of the few trails. Under some spruce I drew up, letting my horses take a breather, and then I saw them. They were at least four hundred feet lower down and perhaps two miles away. They cut across a meadow, loping their horses. The sun glinted on their rifles.

If I went on, my trail would intersect theirs. If I turned back, they would follow. If I tried to hide, they would find me.

My lips were dry. Touching them with my tongue did no good. Taking my canteen, I took a long drink, then stoppered it, watching them. They knew, as I did, that we were close, and I now had an idea who they might be.

The Burrows outfit, and a tough lot. It began to look as if I were riding into trouble, real trouble.

TWENTY-ONE

The Burrows outfit were not like Lew Paine. They were tough, dangerous men who after the killing of their brother Houston would not think of facing me in a man-to-man gun battle. They would try to hunt me down or would lay up somewhere and try an ambush.

Bear Canyon was out in front of me, and the Gold Run Trail, which dipped into it, was not far off. Once in the canyon, a trail led down to the Dolores River and a way out of the area in any direction I chose to go. If that did not seem a good idea, there were at least two trails leading north out of the canyon that would take me to Indian Trail Ridge.

This wasn't country I knew well but I'd heard of the trails. That was the kind of knowledge men passed along to one another. So far the Burrows outfit had been riding a hunch. They had an idea where I was going and they planned to intercept me. If they succeeded in that, it would mean a fight.

Somewhere I would have to make a stand, for if I continued to run they would catch me as they were traveling lighter than I and could move faster.

Riding across the open meadow, I went into the trees and started down the Gold Run Trail, which was a lot of switch-backs, most of them hidden from above by trees. The descent was something over a thousand feet, I judged, and immediately at the bottom I turned west. When I had gone a hundred yards or so I rode into Bear Creek and walked my stock back to the east, keeping in the water until I turned up Grindstone Creek. Then I left the creekbed and took the easternmost of the two trails that went up the mountain. Undoubtedly they were following, and I doubted if my switching from west to east in

148

the creek would fool them for long. It might give me a little advantage and the sort of place I was looking for.

Slowly, anger began to grow in me. This was no trouble I wanted. Houston Burrows had begun it all, and he only got what he expected to give me. These brothers of his felt this was a blood feud, and they had come for me of their own volition. They were hunting me for one reason alone, to kill me. And I was taking them into my country, the high-up mountains where timberline is, where the trees cease to be because their buds are above ground and too easily frozen. The tundra plants that manage to survive have their buds below ground, protected from frost.

Right along that line of timber was where I wanted them. A man could see a great distance up there and hiding places were fewer. Maybe they were high-country people, too, but I doubted it. They were cattlemen and this was sheep country.

Riding out of a dense stand of spruce, I came to an open slope, but riding there was no danger for they could not see me from below if they were following. The blue roan was a mountain horse and seemed to like the high country as much as I did. We were right at ten thousand five hundred feet, judging by the plant growth. My eyes searched my back trail. If they wanted me, they were going to ride some rough country before they got me.

Indian Trail Ridge was above me, above a bare slope of slide rock. Finding a small hollow, I tied my horse to some dwarf spruce, and taking my rifle went up into a tree island of spruce and bellied down.

The spot chosen was perfect. The two trails that came up from different sides of Grindstone Creek met right below me, so no matter which way they came they would be riding in the open, within rifle range. Another trail which I guessed was the Little Bear Trail ran off to the west.

The cluster of Engelmann spruce in which I had taken shelter covered about two acres, quite thick at some points but trailing off in others. There were some lichen-covered rocks among them and some downed timber. My horses were out of sight from the trail they would be following.

If they wanted me, they would find me here. The slow anger that had been growing in me had settled into a bitter, sullen fury. All I'd ever asked was to be let alone.

My back against a tree now, I had a point where both trails

were clearly in view and could rest easy and enjoy myself. The anger was there, but the utter beauty and peace of the country around changed part of it to simple irritation that people would want to bring their blood feuds here.

Down the slight slope before me the earth was scarlet with Indian paintbrush, scattered among it some alpine lilies. On a pile of rock about fifty feet away a yellow-bellied marmot had come out to sun himself. Whether he knew I was there I could not judge, but probably he did not.

They came into view when a good five hundred yards away and I watched them coming. They were expecting trouble, rifles in hand. Resting my Winchester in a fork of the tree before me, I watched them come.

That English lord, he I guided to his hunting, he would have liked this. He was a dry, lonely man who had left his heart somewhere in the Northwest Territories of India. He often spoke of his fighting the Afghans or some others, and of places and times like this. "Our enemies then," he said to me, "but damned fine fighting men. Bold rascals and hard to kill, men who fought for the love of it."

He used to recite Kipling to me, one of the few poets I'd ever read myself.

Those riders down there wanted me dead, but I doubt if they themselves thought of dying. In their dreams it is always the other man who is killed. Well, they would find this was no dream. They'd trailed me into my own country now and I had my back to the wall. Well, to a tree, anyway.

Looking along the rifle barrel, I put my sights on the chest of the nearest man when he was about four hundred yards off, and ever so gently I squeezed off my shot. The rifle jumped in my hands, the sound of the shot racketed against the hills, and the nearest man jerked sharply, then they scattered.

Only there was no place to go. They were out in the open, the nearest cover lying several hundred yards behind them. One man wheeled his horse and lifted his rifle. The trouble was there were several patches of spruce along that gentle slope and some even higher. He didn't know where my shot came from, and he froze, looking.

Taking a piece of cracker from my pack, I bit it off and began to chew. Then I put the rest of it in my mouth, and waited. That rider made a pretty picture, sitting his horse, rifle up, looking. He was some distance off and I just let him sit. My shot had not killed the man at whom I aimed, probably not a serious wound. At least, he had stuck to his saddle.

The sky was blue with scattered tufts of white cloud. The sun was pleasantly warm, the air unbelievably clear. The marmot was gone.

The nearest rider rode back to his companions, and it appeared they were treating or bandaging his wound. At the distance I could not be sure. Leaning back my head, I closed my eyes.

This might be the end of it. Approaching me across the open tundra was asking for a ticket to Boot Hill, but they were vengeful men and would not want to return home to admit failure. They were filled with hatred, obsessed by it.

Sitting up, I watched them. Two remained where they had been but the third started across the wide open area toward the Little Bear Trail. When he reached it he drew up facing me. Puzzled, I watched, glancing from one to the other. Suddenly, as if upon signal, they began riding toward me.

It made no sense. My field of fire was wide open. There was no shelter. In a matter of minutes they would be within range, and they were so far away a concerted rush would be useless. Shifting the rifle, I started to rise.

It was the roan that warned me. The horse snorted suddenly and I looked quickly around.

Three riders had come down the hill behind me, walking their horses, and they were within fifty yards!

Yet, when the roan's snort warned me, they charged. Whipping around, I fired from the hip, saw a man fall, and taking aim I fired again, hearing a thunder of hoofs from behind me.

There was a burst of firing. Lead slashed the trees about me. Leaves fell, a bullet struck the trunk of a spruce and whined off across the grass. Something struck a wicked blow at my leg and it crumpled under me. My hand grasped at a branch and I kept myself from falling but my rifle fell. Shucking my six-shooter, I nailed the first man into the trees, then got off a quick shot at another. He winced but I did not believe I'd more than come close.

The firing ended. On my knees, I ejected two spent shells and reloaded the six-shooter. My rifle had struck a deadfall, bounced, and dropped out of reach beyond it, not more than eight feet away but beyond reach for the moment.

Sweat trickled down my brow and along my nose. My eyes

smarted from it and I wiped a hand across my forehead and eyebrows. Gingerly, my fingers felt for the wound, and found it. Blood had already stained my jeans and left them wet. A bullet seemed to have gone through the back of my thigh but there did not seem to be a broken bone. Pine sap had often been used to stop bleeding, and I believed spruce sap might do as well. There was a deep scar on the side of a tree, and I got sap on my fingers and painted the bullet wounds with it.

Several spruce trees were behind me, their low-hanging boughs sweeping the earth. In the shade of them there was a small bank of dusty snow. Crawling back under the spruce boughs, I got close to the tree trunk. Unless someone parted the boughs I was invisible. Anyone who tried that would get a bullet where it mattered. Waiting, I listened.

In the clear mountain air, voices carried. ". . . Got him, I tell you! Seen him fall!"

"He's a tough one."

"Bah! He's down! He's done for! I know I hit him!"

"I saw him fall," another said, "but I'm not going in there after him. I'd as soon tackle a wounded grizzly."

"We don't have to go in after him. We just ride off an' wait. If he doesn't come out, we nailed him. It's simple as that."

"Take his horses, too. Don't leave nothin'."

"Not that roan! That's the Death Horse. Now it's been the death of him, too."

"We won't keep him, just lead him away from here. I don't want it, either."

Either their voices faded or I did, because I heard nothing more. Slowly, very carefully, I stretched out my wounded leg. Whatever I needed was on my packhorse and they were taking it away. It would be dark before long, and cold. It would be bitter cold as I was right at eleven thousand feet or better, and a fire would be an invitation for them to come back and finish me.

With my hands I dug a hollow in the thick bed of needles fallen among the trees. With my knife I cut boughs from the spruce and then I lay back, pulling the thick spruce boughs over me. They would not help much but I needed all I could get. It was going to be a bad night, a very bad night.

Cold was the moon rising over Orphan Butte, still crested with last winter's snow, and cold the wind that whispered through the spruce and stirred the Indian paintbrush on the meadow. It was an empty world, and at night, nothing moved. Up here a slight wind could drop the chill factor by thirty degrees, and the Burrows outfit were not used to high country. No doubt they had been up this high, but not often. They had made their camp in a little draw below a peak this side of Grindstone Lake. Their fire could easily be seen.

If they'd been used to high country they would have known subalpine valleys were the coldest places, for as the thin air chills it flows down, leaving the tundra somewhat warmer.

Lying back in my little trough, I covered myself with debris from the trees around me and with the spruce boughs again. I was weak, I was hurting, and it was cold, icy, bitter cold.

Because of their presence I had to endure it, but that was also an advantage, for they did not have to endure. They could pick up and leave, and I knew they would.

Slow passed the moonlit night, slow came the dawn, and rising to an elbow I could see them stirring about their fire. They would be arguing the point now but I knew they were not up to a second night here. Light reflected from a glass. They were studying the island of spruce through a field glass. At the distance I could have killed him, but it would have started the fight all over again and I was in no shape for it.

Barely recovered from one gunshot wound I now had another, and staring up into the growing light I took stock and saw no light at the end of this tunnel. Even if they rode away now, what could I do? Any help I might get was miles away over rough country, and the chances of anybody else being up this high was remote.

After a bit I sat up again and when I looked toward their camp there was nothing there.

Nothing, because they were coming toward me. They were scattered out and they were coming. One of them, trailing behind, had a body over a saddle. So I'd gotten one of them, anyway.

They came on toward me and I rolled myself over, careful to stir nothing they could see, and I crawled to my rifle. Then I waited.

When they got within two hundred yards they pulled up, then slowly began to circle my hideout, studying the grass. They wanted to see if I'd moved during the night and left some sign. They found none. Then they drew up, looking toward me.

There had been six in all. One was dead, two wounded, although neither seriously.

Waiting, I rested my rifle in the notch of a tree and decided which was to die first. Their voices were inaudible. Finally they turned their horses and rode away, driving my stock ahead of them. When they disappeared from sight down the Bear Creek Trail, I lay back on the spruce needles and closed my eyes.

For a long time I just rested, thinking of nothing, content to be alone, not to have to worry about the next attack. At last my eyes opened and I looked up to the blue sky overhead and watched a cloud drift slowly across the blue. If I died here, they would have won and I should have failed in whatever I wanted to do or be. And it was not in me to quit. Oh, I could lose! I'd lost before this, but quit?

No.

Had they actually gone? For a little longer I waited, then I came out of the spruce island on the uphill side and crawled away, keeping to low ground. There was no chance of concealing my movements in the growth, for the flowers and other tundra plants were all low, close to the ground. There were places where the flowers grew up to a foot or eighteen inches, but they were very scattered and sparse in that area. With about a quarter of a mile behind me, I got hold of some rocks and pulled myself erect. My leg hurt abominably when I tried to walk, but I hobbled a few steps. Rested, easing the pain, and then I struggled on a few steps further.

After a while, coming to some flat, lichen-covered rocks, I rested. Thunder rumbled in the distance. Often there were thunderstorms every afternoon in the mountains, and desperately I hoped this would not be one. Lightning is an ever-present danger at high altitudes, and I was carrying a rifle.

Rising from the rock where I rested, I hobbled on, using the rifle as a staff. That time I made fifty yards before I had to stop.

After a rest, I started on, feeling faint and sick. There was another stand of forest just before me and somehow I kept going, then I fell. With my last strength I dragged myself into the partial shade of some spruce. Reaching out to crawl a little further, I faded out.

A spatter of raindrops brought me to awareness, but it was already dark. With an effort I dragged myself and my rifle into the cover of the spruce trees, and then consciousness ebbed again. All I heard was distant thunder and the sound of rain.

TWENTY-TWO

Rolling over, I got my hands under me and began to crawl, reaching back for my rifle. It was slightly uphill, but I made it to the shelter of another spruce and lay under its protecting boughs, shivering and cold.

Wrapping my arms around myself, I simply lay and shuddered. There was nothing I could do, the spruce kept the rain off me, but nothing kept out the cold and I was wet and sick.

Long stretched the night, and cold and wet I longed for the dawn. My mouth was dry and I opened it to catch occasional drops. I had to get out of here. I had to get down where it was warmer, and at last the long night passed and my eyes saw a faint yellow in the sky, and then, exhausted beyond belief, I slept at last.

When I awakened it was full day, and for a time I simply lay still, only half-awake. Then I struggled and sat up, looking around. My hat lay on the needles near me and I put it on my head. My rifle lay beside me, and almost automatically and without thinking I took it up and wiped it dry with my bandanna. On an almost flat rock a few feet away there was a small pool of water, gathered from the rain. Crawling over, I sucked it up, then sat back and closed my eyes again.

For a long time I merely sat, enjoying the sun. It was warm and pleasant. Then awareness began to return. It was warm now, but in a few hours there would be piercing cold again. If I were going to get off the mountain, I must start.

Yet I did not move. Tilting my head back, I soaked up the warmth, feeling the stiffness slowly leaving my muscles. When I began to move I was almost unconscious of it. Some inner drive for survival started me and pushed me on. Using a stick found in the debris around the spruce trees, I hobbled down the slope, found the Little Bear Trail, and started along it.

The yellow-bellied marmot was out on his rocks to see me go, nose twitching. He whistled sharply when I first moved, then simply watched as if aware I was no problem demanding attention. Dully I thought this was no different than a few days ago on the ridge back of the ranch. Then cold realization seeped into my consciousness. It was different. It was very different. Here there was no welcoming ranch, no bunk, no waiting rest and comfort. All that was miles away, miles of forest, streams, brush, deadfalls, slide rock, and in all that vast area, nobody.

Yet, the movement had its effect. Slow though it was, my blood began to circulate and consciousness returned.

Janet Le Caudy had gone to Durango. She had an aunt there. Reed Bell was planning to arrest Mrs. Hollyrood, Clinton, and Matty as soon as the sheriff returned. In the meantime, they were still at large.

Would they give up and try to evade capture? Or did they know the law was coming for them? From their standpoint they had only two problems, Janet and me. Without Janet they might make their will stand as the rightful one and still keep title to the ranch. That also meant eliminating me as a witness, but I was certain now that my elimination had been planned all along so she could have whatever money I had left from my stake.

By nightfall I had covered scarcely more than a mile. Yet now I could build a fire, and I did. A small shelter against a cutbank, using it as reflector for my fire. Gradually as the evening drew on, I made my fire longer until it was burning over a good six feet, and when I decided it had been burning long enough I moved the fire over, brought it back to a reasonable size, and after making sure no burning coals remained, stretched out on the warm ground where the fire had been.

At daybreak I awakened feeling much rested. Again I started, but this time when the trail divided I took the lower, which followed the creek. My loss of blood and general weakness had left me thirsty and I could drink as often as I wished.

Badly wounded, I dared not try to remain where I was. To stay here was to die. It was as simple as that. Snow could begin falling at any time at this altitude and this time of year, and if it did there was a good chance I'd never get out. It was late September and the leaves had started turning on the aspen.

Nobody ever told me life was easy, and for me it had never been, but I was, I think, the stronger because of it. One learns to succeed by succeeding in small things first. Mostly a person learns to succeed by simply overcoming failure.

Getting down the mountain couldn't be done by wishing, and the chances of anybody finding me were slight. Besides, who would look? Most of the folks I knew figured I'd left the country, and the others wished I had.

Yet I did have one hope, one chance I could think of for help, but it was neither man nor woman. It was that blue roan. He had found me once before. Of course, that was only within a few yards, but he had come looking. Where the Burrows boys had driven my stock, I don't know. I doubted they'd drive it far because they'd not want to be seen with my stock in the event the law started making queries. Somebody, sooner or later, would find my body and that would start talk, so they'd get shut of those horses soon as they could. And that blue roan an' me, well, we'd developed a feelin' for each other.

Nevertheless, a thing like that couldn't be depended upon, so I just kept hobbling along, never looking back because I knew the sight of how little I'd done would discourage me. My eyes were on the trail ahead, as they'd always been.

The sun was warm, even down in the canyon, and I worked along, taking my time, content with every foot I made, not thinking of all the miles yet to be done.

Mostly it was downhill, which helped. Now and again I rested. Sure, I was hungry, but I'd been hungry before. I'd ridden that trail many a time in my years, often because I just didn't have the money to buy food, just as often because I wasn't where it could be had.

Walking in the bottom of the canyon, I did not notice when the sky began to overcast. By that time I'd come out of Little Bear into Bear Canyon and was headed downstream. Somewhere ahead should be the Dolores River, and there was a well-traveled trail alongside the river. I did notice when the snow began to fall.

It came down easy, there at first. Just a few lazy, drifting flakes that landed and melted as they landed. I felt ghostly wet fingers of snow touch my cheek. Weak as a cat, I just sat down on a rock. I sat down and leaned my forearms on my thighs, easing my wounded leg a bit.

It seemed like the last straw. Snow could pile up pretty fast in these canyons.

The rocks underfoot would be slippery and travel that much harder. Getting up, I started on. It was snowing steady now, a lazy fall of big flakes but they did not stop. Judging by the growth, I was down to a bit over eight thousand feet, and the Dolores Trail couldn't be more than a mile or two further along.

Brushing the snow from a fallen log, I sat down. My legs wouldn't stop trembling. The thought came that I should build a fire but I shook it off. The Dolores Trail could not be far ahead, not that it promised much because I'd still be a long way from anywhere.

It was cold, and getting colder. All I had was my suit coat and vest. One leg of my jeans was stiff with dried blood, and I felt weak and sick. My fingers fumbled at my face. A stubble of beard. Looking at my hand, I saw it trembling and closed it tight into a fist to stop it.

After a moment, growing colder, I struggled to my feet, swayed a bit, then started on.

How much farther I got, I don't know. Somehow my foot tripped over a root and I fell face-down in the fresh snow. I remembered trying to get up, but my leg hurt something awful and I just passed out.

The next thing I knew I was lying on a bed and somebody was working over me. My eyes opened and all I could realize was the softness of that bed compared to frozen ground, and that I was warm. When I looked around I saw the person working on me was an Indian woman. As I was trying to turn over, she put a hard hand on my shoulder and pushed me back, saying something in Ute. I looked at her again, and it was the woman whose man I'd buried back along the trail, the one who cut me down when I was hanged.

She spoke and two Ute men came in from the next room along with a white man and, of all things, Janet Le Caudy.

"You're awake!" she exclaimed.

"Seems like," I said, "although you're a dream."

She flushed and looked impatient. "We had an awful time finding you, and if it hadn't been for the Utes we never would have.

"It seems," she commented, "you did something for them at some time."

Well, I didn't respond to that except to say they were good folks and they'd done something for me, too. And how did she get here, anyway?

"Your horses came back to town. I think they were on the way to the ranch. I knew something had happened, but nobody would come with me to look for you. They said it was going to snow and we'd be trapped in the high country. Anyway, they said you'd be dead or your horses wouldn't have come back all saddled and packed.

"The Dutchman saw the Burrows boys go through with a couple of wounded men and another across a saddle. Then when your horses showed up he was sure they had killed you. I didn't believe it so I went to the Utes."

"Why them? What made you—"

"My uncle knew them and traded with them. He liked them. I grew up speaking their language, too, so when I went to them for help, they listened. And when I told them you were riding the blue roan they seemed to know who you were."

"We met one time."

"We caught your horses and backtracked them, then lost the trail. The Utes said you would come down Bear Creek, so we tried that and found you."

"Where are we now?"

"In a ranch house. You were only about a mile from it when you fell."

We were silent for a while, and the Utes left the room and I could hear some stirring around and smell coffee. Suddenly I was hungry, but hungry as I was I just didn't want to even move. I just wanted to lie there and rest. There was another voice and I asked who it was.

"We're at a ranch house. It's the owner. At least, the man who is living here."

All in as I was, I fell asleep again, and when I opened my eyes, on the chair beside the bed was a fresh pair of my own jeans and one of the new shirts I'd bought. Janet had evidently gotten them from my pack. So I got dressed.

The Utes were gone but Janet was there. I dropped into a chair, exhausted by the few feet I'd walked from the bed. She brought me coffee.

"You speak *Ute?* I thought you were eastern?"

"I lived with my aunt and uncle out here for a while when I was very young. I played with Ute children."

Over coffee she brought me up-to-date. "Reed Bell and the sheriff went out to the ranch, and they arrested Mrs. Hollyrood. It seems under that gray wig that was always done so beautifully that she's a brunette."

"Somebody said she was a blonde. I heard the woman Bell was looking for was a—"

"Blonde? She was, but women bleach their hair or dye it." She smiled at me. "Few women are content with what they are or how they look. They always seem to think a change is for the better."

Well, I could believe that, little as I knew about womenfolks. They did always seem to be switching things around. Men are more often content with what is familiar, in their homes, anyway.

Janet brought me up-to-date on some things. Nobody had seen Clinton. The general idea was that he had left the country. Nobody had anything on him, anyway. That he had tried to keep Janet a prisoner was something that could not be proved. She had gone to the ranch willingly, and there just wasn't any solid evidence against him. Nor was there anything against Matty. They might try to get her for aiding and abetting, but I was prepared to testify she had warned me away and had objected to what was being planned by Mrs. Hollyrood.

"We've got to get back," Janet said. "I was frightened for you and came away when I should be in Parrott City or at the ranch."

"Tomorrow," I said.

My leg wasn't in as bad shape as a body would suspect, and that Indian woman, she put some kind of a poultice on it made from herbs.

What I needed most was just rest, and I slept most of the day and all night. Come daylight I rolled out. I was never much on lyin' abed anyway. Always wanted to be up an' doin', so I took my time dressing, ate a quick breakfast, and got into the saddle. There were three Ute men and the woman, and they rode alongside as we started back.

When we finally rode into Parrott I was used up. We'd camped out along the way, and I was surely glad to have the Utes along because, weak as I was, I certainly wasn't of much account. When we started up La Plata Canyon the Utes rode off, and we came into town, just the two of us.

The Dutchman was dipping red-hot iron into his tank when we rode by, and he just straightened up and looked, but he had nothing to say. Some men got up from their benches along the storefronts and walked to the edge of the boardwalk to look. Most of them never moved at all.

Cookie looked up when we came in to eat and brought coffee to the table. "You look kind of wore out," he commented. "Somebody treat you bad?"

"Kind of," I said. "It's gettin' cold in the mountains."

"Saw the Burrows boys ride through. Had a body over a saddle."

"Well, what d'you know? They must have run into trouble."

"They looked kind of beat up and shot up."

"I don't know what the young folks are comin' to, these days. All kinds of gallivantin' about. Restless, that's what they are, restless. They ought to have more chores to do."

Saw some of the usual faces around and some strangers, miners, mostly. Men rustlin' work in some of the holes up on the mountains. There at the table I took out that other will and gave it to Janet. She stared at it, then tears came into her eyes. "It was like him," she said. "I could never believe he had disowned me."

"Half the ranch was yours, anyway."

We ate in silence there for a while, and folks came and went around us. Each of us busy with thinking what we were going to do, I expect. At least, I was.

It was time to light a shuck for the high country. No sooner had I told myself that than I recalled it was too late in the season and it would be right chilly up there. The high country would have to wait for another year. Anyway, there was Phoenix, that Arizona town named by the Englishman, Darrell Duppa.

Phoenix, like the bird it was named for, was rising from the ashes of an ancient town built by the Hohokam or some such people. It would be warm and pleasant down thataway, a place for a lone-riding man to live out the cold months.

"You'll be workin' the ranch?" I asked.

"Of course. I love the place. It needs work but nothing that I can't get done with a couple of good hands." She looked at me out of those blue eyes, and I looked away real quick. "And you?" she asked.

"I was just passin' through when I rode in here, so I reckon I'll just tip my hat to the hills, roll up my ball of yarn, an' keep on passin'."

She looked right at me then, and she said, "I don't want you to go."

No woman ever said that to me before.

TWENTY-THREE

Well, I was scared. Looking across the table I said, "Ma'am, I'd like to stay but I'd be a nuisance. I never had much truck with womenfolks. I'm just a driftin' man, draggin' his spurs ever' which way. I don't know much but horses, cattle, an' country rock."

She put her hand over mine. "Mr. Passin', I want you to stay. I don't want you to leave, ever."

For a moment there I couldn't speak. Who was I to deserve the likes of her?

"Well," I said, "there's a lot of high-up hills right close around here."

"And when you want to go," she said, "if you want, I'll go with you."

That was the way it was, and when I'd taken her back to the hotel I went to the store and bought myself a set of hand-me-downs. I mean, I bought a suit right off the shelf. There was no tailor in town but I'd never had a tailored suit anyway. Fact is, I'd never had a suit before, not since Pa bought me one when I was knee-high, and that was for goin' to church an' such.

We'd talked it out, and we'd be married right there in Parrott City and ride back to the ranch together.

When I came back on the street with that package under my left arm, who should be standing there but Matty. She stood there, her hair blowing a little in the wind, all alone.

"Matty," I said, walking over to her, "what are you going to do now?"

"Mrs. Hollyrood was arrested."

"I know."

"She intended to poison you. I didn't want that to happen. You're a good man."

"Have you got any money, Matty? Remember, we're friends."

"I have nothing. They took it all, although there wasn't much."

Aside from my walking-around money I still had twelve hundred dollars. I'd bought an expensive suit, paid fifteen dollars for it. Reaching down in my jeans, I took out a hundred dollars.

"I can't take that."

"We're friends, Matty. Go someplace, get a fresh start. You'll do all right. Just believe in yourself."

She took the money. "Thank you, Mr. Passin'. I'll not forget this."

"Don't worry about it."

She turned away. "Matty?" I said. She looked around. "What's your other name? Matty what?"

"Higgins," she said, then after a pause, "I'm a Clinch Mountain Higgins."

She walked away down the street toward the stage station and I watched her go. She was a truly beautiful woman.

At the hotel I switched into that new suit, and had me a struggle with the necktie. Reminded me of a cowboy I'd heard of. The first time they put a tie on his neck he didn't move for two days. Thought he was tied to a hitchin' post.

The Dutchman had rounded up a sky pilot and some folks gathered around to be at the wedding. With my collar all cinched up like that I hadn't been so strangled since they tried to hang me that time.

That sky pilot brought the Good Book with him and we stood up whilst he spoke the words, and simple as that, I was a married man with a beautiful wife, so while she talked with womenfolks, the Dutchman and me went out to saddle our horses.

That blue roan was standing ready and I saddled my other horse for Janet. I'd finished cinching up and walked around the horse when the Dutchman spoke.

"Mr. Passin'? Watch it."

Well, I looked around, and across the street stood Charles Pelham Clinton in a white suit and a panama hat and he was standing there looking across at me.

"I've been looking for you, Mr. Passin'," he said quietly. "I've been looking and waiting."

"I'm here," I said.

"You surprised me," he said, "and I didn't expect it of you. You seem to have a gift for survival."

Now Charles Pelham Clinton, whose brother I'd killed and whose plans I'd helped to upset, had not come to talk about politics or the weather, nor even to congratulate me on my wedding. But maybe he did.

"You're a bridegroom, I hear," Clinton said, "and you married Janet Le Caudy, of all people."

"I did."

"Too bad," he said, "for such a young wife to become a widow."

"It would be," I replied.

"But," he said, "I must congratulate you. In fact I must take off my hat to you." He lifted his hand to his hat and then his hand started down and I shot him dead.

The Dutchman started forward. "You shot him! You—!"

"Look in his hand," I said.

Clinton lay sprawled, one hand outstretched, one almost under him. In the palm of his right hand was a double-barreled .44 derringer.